Peggy S Regel

The Senator's Wife's Deception

PEGGY S. REGEL

Order this book online at www.trafford.com/07-2085
or email orders@trafford.com

Most Trafford titles are also available at major online book retailers.

Note for Librarians: A cataloguing record for this book is available from Library
and Archives Canada at www.collectionscanada.ca/amicus/index-e.html

Printed in Victoria, BC, Canada.

ISBN: 978-1-4251-4830-0

*We at Trafford believe that it is the responsibility of us all, as both individuals and corporations,
to make choices that are environmentally and socially sound. You, in turn, are supporting this
responsible conduct each time you purchase a Trafford book, or make use of our publishing services.
To find out how you are helping, please visit www.trafford.com/responsiblepublishing.html*

*Our mission is to efficiently provide the world's finest, most comprehensive book publishing
service, enabling every author to experience success. To find out how to publish your book, your
way, and have it available worldwide, visit us online at www.trafford.com/10510*

Trafford
PUBLISHING™ www.trafford.com

North America & international
toll-free: 1 888 232 4444 (USA & Canada)
phone: 250 383 6864 ♦ fax: 250 383 6804 ♦ email: info@trafford.com

The United Kingdom & Europe
phone: +44 (0)1865 722 113 ♦ local rate: 0845 230 9601
facsimile: +44 (0)1865 722 868 ♦ email: info.uk@trafford.com

10 9 8 7 6 5 4 3

DEDICATION

My loving husband "Scotty"
without whose encouragement
and support
I would not have been able
to write this novel.

1

THE BEGINNING

Betty was aggravated. Damn this snow storm. It had been hard enough for her to decide to return to Washington and to her marriage to Senator Stewart. Leaving Denver at 6 A.M. was no joke in itself, but they had a delay in flight. They were forced to land in Oklahoma City and from there another delay in St. Louis. The storm had again held their flight an additional hour. Not only was the breakfast a nightmare on the plane, morning sickness was not mental, she reminded herself. Throwing up in that tiny bathroom was difficult and humiliating.

It was already past lunchtime and she should have been in Washington. Would she lose her nerve?

Calling the stewardess, Betty ordered another cocktail. She knew she had already had more than her share, but her courage was faltering. When she had left Denver this morning, her father had assured her that returning to her husband was the best decision she would ever make.

Sipping the cocktail, Betty's head was filled with past memories of her marriage. Jason was a dear man, he just wasn't her ideal of a husband. He was handsome, intelligent, kind, considerate and generous. Even though she knew her drinking embarrassed him at political dinners and functions, he never scolded her. Jason, thought Betty, was a dull nothing. Moving into a separate bedroom had been her ideal and as usual, Jason consented. Rarely, and only if she initiated it, did they even have intercourse.

Tears blurred her vision as she thought about returning to this life. A life that was a shell. Jason would never consent to a divorce and now that she was pregnant, the baby would need a father. A faint smile came to her lips as she thought of the baby. Poor Jason, she thought. When she had called him and told him that she was pregnant, he was elated. Naturally he would be. He was so damned noble.

The baby would force her to continue the charade of a happy and successful life. The papers would print pictures of the darling Senator from Georgia and his wife with their new baby. Thank God she wouldn't have to take care of it. Nothing about the baby interested her. She had to endure the pregnancy and for this she would never forgive her father. Daisy would give the child the love and guidance it would need or they could hire a full time nanny.

Finding her drink empty, she again paged the stewardess.

Nancy Riddle had seen some lushes in her life, but the woman in the first class section was the prize. If the storm lasted much longer, this passenger wouldn't be able to stand when they reached their destination at National. When she saw which button had been pushed, she took extra time in responding. It was obvious what she wanted. Rich bitch, thought Nancy. Her mannerism and clothes suggested this woman had money behind her. The diamond ring on her finger probably cost more than Nancy made in a year or two. She was listed on the manifest as Betty Stewart, wife of Senator Jason Stewart from Georgia. Looking back, Nancy could see that the woman was beautiful. She was slender, had beautiful bleached hair and her makeup was done with taste.

All she had done since she boarded this flight was bitch. First, she couldn't get a window seat. This slight, she took personally. Of course, her reservation hadn't been made until the night before. She was fortunate to get in the first class section at all. A salesman from Philadelphia had canceled just as Mrs. Stewart called for a reservation.

With a sigh, Nancy placed the drink on the tray and took it to Mrs. Stewart. Betty asked the usual question that Nancy had answered at least 20 times on her way from the galley. The storm had delayed them indefinitely. However, there must be a break in the weather, as the decision to board passengers from St. Louis was going to start in just a few minutes. This was a positive sign.

Betty had mixed feelings. She wanted to get on with her life. Had she made the right decision to return to Washington and Jason? How many choices did she have, she thought bitterly. God how she had tried to love Jason. He really was a good man. Too good for her, an inner voice said. Could she continue living the deception of a dutiful wife and later, a loving mother? Would Jason ever know her secret? In her present state of mind, she even felt a little smug that once in her life, she had managed to outsmart Jason. What would he do if he ever found out?

On the advice of her father, she had decided not to tell Sam about the baby. Her father had never liked Sam. Yet, if Betty ever knew love, it was her feeling for Sam. Was she the loser in this triangle or was Sam? She wondered.

This thought process was interrupted by the discharging and boarding of passengers. Betty hoped that whomever had the window seat would have changed their mind or their reservation. She did love the window seat. If the person next to her was boring or if she didn't want to be engaged in conversation she could simply turn away and pretend interest in the landscapes below. With this storm though, all she had seen so far from her aisle seat, was clouds and blowing snow.

2

APRIL AND BETTY

April leaned back in her seat on the 747 with a heavy heart. TWA Flight 406 would take her from this small town in Missouri to the Nation's Capitol where she would become a government employee like thousands of other young women. "If only I can pass the physical without having my pregnancy detected," she thought. Tears filled her eyes as she thought about Max. When she had told him about the baby, his reaction was hardly what she had expected. "Hadn't she realized that coming out with that kind of news at this particular time could hurt his chances in the upcoming election. He had worked too hard to lose it all now," he had said. "Besides, he hated telling her like this, but he was going to announce his engagement to Serena, a wealthy Missouri businessman's daughter shortly. He was sorry, but a baby was out of the question at this time and suggested an abortion." He had kept talking, but April heard nothing else. Her whole world had just fallen apart. True he had been distant lately, but with the election snowballing as it was, she had attributed this to the demands on his time. Never in her whole life, would she have thought that Max would desert her like this. Her and his baby.

As the plane lifted off, she shut her eyes but the picture of Max's face would not fade. No matter how she tried, April could not erase the tender smile, forget his loving touch or cast out of her mind the promises and plans they had made together. That was all before Serena came into the picture. Serena was beautiful, poised and had connections that would be beneficial to Max in his bid for a congressional position.

April remembered how infatuated Max had been when he first saw Serena. She truly was a vision of loveliness. Yet, never in her wildest dreams would she have thought Max would toss her over for Serena. She and Max had grown up together, shared first date, kiss, high school, college, and sexual experiences. Now she regretted ever allowing herself to be so stupid as to get pregnant. She had tried birth control pills but they made her so ill. Max had promised to use something. Obviously he didn't. She thought of how she had worked so diligently behind the scenes to help Max get his name on the ballot for Congressman. He was the all American type. Tall, handsome, honest and ambitious. Everything he touched or attempted, was a success. Now this.

Max had used her. She had assisted in his speech writing, researched material long into the wee hours, and taken poll after poll on political opinions. With these polls, she had suggested several issues to Max that needed to be included in his campaign. There was no doubt that she put as much or more into this campaign as Max himself. It had meant their working side by side and they spent long days and short nights together. There was never a reason for her to doubt that it wouldn't lead to anything less than marriage. The only mistake she had made was yielding to his sexual demands. It wasn't that their lovemaking hadn't been great, it was. But when she discovered that she was pregnant, her wildest dream never included Max dumping her for another woman. The town of St. Joseph had been their downfall. There Max met and fell head over heels in love with Serena.

Feeling close to tears, April got up from her seat to go to the rest room. The young woman sitting beside her had only been a blur until now. Getting up from her seat so April would not have to climb over, it was obvious at one glance that this young woman had the poise, grace and breeding of old money. Her clothes were not over done but stylish and worn with confidence. Until now, they had only said hello. April noticed that they were approximately the same height and similar blond hair. There was no doubt that they were the same dress size and April would have killed to afford clothes like Betty was wearing. Even though the suit Betty wore was tailored, it reeked dollars. An original design, no less.

April used the bathroom and splashed water on her face. She thought all the tears had been cried out. Probably, she thought, there would be a lifetime of tears. The ache was so real. She simply couldn't admit that she had lost Max. Her whole life had been devoted to his wishes and dreams. Never once had there been a hint that his goals would not include her.

Returning to her seat, April saw that the young woman had moved over to the window seat, allowing her to sit on the aisle.

"I do hope you don't mind. Every time I make this trip, I try to capture the beauty of Washington, D.C. from the air. It never ceases to thrill me," she said.

Seeing that April was not going to open up, Betty tried again.

"I don't believe I introduced myself. I am Betty Stewart. Since we are going to have several hours together, perhaps you would like to talk."

April turned and took Betty's hand. "I am April Simmons. I'm on my way to Washington to work for the government." As they chatted, April couldn't help but notice that the woman was slurring her words. She had obviously had too much to drink.

"That's how I met my husband," said Betty. "Right out of college I went straight to Washington. My father went to medical school with a political activist from Georgia. His friend didn't make it as a surgeon but said anyone could be successful in politics. So through his assistance I became a stenographer/administrative aid in the Senate. A really small fish in a big pond."

"Most people think politics are reserved for the elected forces. Let me tell you, the steno and administrative pool is all politics. No unknown girl, no matter how good she is, gets to even come in contact with the "royal senators" unless the dragon lady in charge decides. I have come to the absolute conclusion that all frustrated, dumpy, ugly and slightly demented old maid's are in charge of these pools. Their one ambition in life it to serve their country well and make young girls lives miserable."

April and Betty both laughed at this.

Betty continued. "One day, during one of the famous Washington snow storms, I was dumb enough to show up for work. It wasn't loyalty mind you, it was stupidity. I just simply didn't know that the city shut down during this type of weather. Anyway, I showed up for work and found that I was all alone in the office. All the other help called in with excuses. The telephone rang off the hook. Now I have often wondered who these people thought was going to take these calls as over half of the city was snuggled deep into their blankets and enjoying this short reprieve from work. Anyway, as luck or fate would have it, I was sitting at Ms. Shoney's desk when the Senator arrived. He swept into the office with snow all over his beautiful expensive overcoat and boots. Immediately I jumped up and offered to help brush the snow from his clothing. I was totally unaware that he was taking a good long hard look at me. One thing I do know though is that my own heart was racing a mile a minute. I was within a breath of this young Senator from Georgia and totally enchanted."

"He asked me how I made it to work and I simply told him that I had walked. My car was covered with snow and the plow had made it impossible to get out of my parking spot. There are no buses and the taxi's were all full. On Pennsylvania Avenue, half way to work I had broken the heel on my shoe when I slipped. Being from Boulder, you would have thought I'd have worn my snow boots, but they weren't unpacked yet. Other than that, there had been no real problems."

"Can you believe he asked me to have lunch with him? Naturally I said yes. The morning just dragged as I watched the clock climb slowly to twelve. He took me to the dining room in the capitol building. To this day I can't remember what we ate."

"When I got back to the office I found a new pair of shoes on my desk. He had sent his driver downtown to purchase them for me. When the day ended, I was surprised to find him again in front of Ms. Shoney's desk."

"He said it was still snowing and that he and his driver would be happy to take me home. That is, if I would consent to have dinner with him. To this day I don't know why I felt a little apprehensive. Maybe it was because he suggested his place. With the whole town shut down, the best restaurants were closed. He assured me he had a devoted housekeeper and that I would be perfectly safe. I don't remember for sure, but I must have said yes. Anyway, one thing led to another and we were finally married and have been for four years now."

April asked Betty where she was coming from. Betty had stated that her father was a surgeon in Boulder and since she hadn't been feeling too well she flew home for a checkup. "When I discovered I was pregnant, I called Jason and he told me to catch the next plane out of Boulder and come home for a celebration." April did not catch the sarcasm in Betty's voice. She was an expert at hiding her feelings.

Betty ordered another drink and tears ran down her cheeks as she continued. "You see, I never wanted children. When I thought I was pregnant, our marriage had gotten a little stale and I needed to get away for a little while. Naturally, I flew home to my father. In all his wisdom, he told me to tell Jason about the baby and to try and put the spark back into our marriage." Drunk as she was, Betty amazed herself in making her story sound so normal. She hated being pregnant, she hated her father, Jason and Sam. Most of all, she hated herself for getting into this mess.

Betty's voice lowered as she said softly, "Jason was so happy about the baby on the telephone. I got goose bumps from his enthusiasm. Then this darn storm forced my plane to fly into St. Louis. So far, I drove from Boulder to Denver at 4 A.M. this morning, got grounded in Oklahoma City and again in St. Louis. For a direct flight, it has taken forever to finally get close to my destination of National. My patience can endure only so much. The celebration will have to wait. I'm so worn out now, all I want is my warm bed and a cup of Daisy's coffee." This was said in a spoiled, whiney voice.

Betty turned to April and said, "My word, I apologize for rambling on about myself. Perhaps I have bored you. Please tell me something about yourself."

Just as April started to relate her brief history about working to get Max Hartley elected congressman from Missouri, there was a shudder and flashing lights came on. The stewardess' were giving instructions about fastening seat belts and passing out pillows for people to place in their laps. Warnings were given about dousing all cigarettes and removing all eyeglasses. They were in the air space over Washington and the landing gear was locked or frozen in place. The wheels would not come down! The fuel was low but the pilot was confident he could set the plane down. They were going in for an emergency landing!

April felt something move beside her. Betty had slipped her hand over the divider in the seats and was seeking April's hand. The look on Betty's face was one of total despair. April saw that Betty was crying and asking God to forgive her. She was babbling in her drunken state about how sorry she was for treating Jason so badly. Finally April put her head down on the pillow, saying her own prayers.

The next thing April remembered was someone pulling her from a dark cold and hot twisted mass of metal and jamming a needle into her arm. Pain besieged her body. When she tried to cry out, she couldn't. Her mouth felt as if it had been separated from her head. She had difficulty breathing and tried to feel her nose. Her arms weighed thousands of pounds. Only one word was uttered in the ambulance, but it was inaudible. "Betty!"

3

WAKING UP

When April woke, she found that she could not move. She was in a strange place and everything seemed foreign to her. Even more frightening was the fact that she could not move, nor speak.

A nurse sitting beside her bed noticed her stirring and stood up. Touching April's hand, she began talking softly. "My dear, don't try to move or talk. You have been in a terrible accident. You are in George Washington Hospital and we are doing everything we can to make you well. You are one lucky survivor. I would hate to think what might have been if your husband hadn't defied all the firemen and rescue workers. That crazy Senator plunged into that burning plane and pulled you out with his bare hands. He got some burns himself, but nothing serious. Try to relax and I'll go get the doctor."

As the doctor entered the room, he was again shocked to see this patient. Her chances of survival had been less than 50% when she was brought into the emergency room. Putting on his best doctor's smile, he walked over to April's bedside and took her hand. Patting it, he began to talk to her. There was terror in her eyes.

"Mrs. Stewart, you are one lucky woman. We have been waiting for five days to have you wake up and talk to us. If you remember, you were in a plane crash right off the tip of the runway at National. You were brought to us with a broken collarbone, broken left arm and leg. Both your jaws are broken and wired. Your nose was almost severed from your face and naturally there are multiple cuts and bruises all over your body. All of your teeth were knocked out or broken off."

"We thought at first, because of the impact of the crash and the abrasions to your face and head that there might have been some brain damage. However an EEG shown only minimal swelling. We don't expect any permanent damage. At most, some memory loss. Your body took some pretty bad burns and your face was badly cut. Now that you are awake, we can start scheduling you for some corrective surgery. Can't seem to figure out what hit you in the mouth. Your teeth were broken off even with the gums. We'll have to extract them and dental has been alerted to stop in and take impressions. First, we need to get you into surgery and reconstruct your face. Your nose had to be sewn back on and your jaws and chin reshaped. Fortunately there was no damage to your eyes. All in all, Mrs. Stewart, you are one lucky person. You are young, healthy and alive."

"Now if you would like some company, your husband has been walking the halls here since he brought you in. I can only allow him a minute, but a visit will be good for both of you." Saying this, the doctor left the room.

Shortly, a tall, dark headed handsome man entered the room. He looked as though he hadn't slept for a week. His chin was covered with an unruly growth. His hair was disheveled and his eyes had large circles under them. Nevertheless, he was a handsome figure.

Rushing over to April's bed, the man took her hand and kissed it. There were tears in his eyes. "Baby, everything is going to be all right. Thank God you were spared. We still don't know about the baby. We can always have another one if this one doesn't survive. Oh Betty, you are my life, please get well and come home with me. I can't imagine life without you."

April was bewildered. Suddenly it dawned on her that this was Jason Stewart, Betty's husband. Oh no, she thought. He thinks I'm Betty. Oh God, I must tell him the truth.

Gesturing with her hand that wasn't casted, but taped to a board with tubes running everywhere, she tried to convey to Senator Stewart that she was not his wife. Sounds came from her mouth, but they were inaudible because her jaws were wired and her face with the exception of her eyes was casted. Desperately she tried to tell the Senator who she was. The nurse standing by saw how upset April had become and walked over to the Senator. Asking him to leave, she inserted the needle into the tube and April drifted into dreamland once again.

Most of the time spent in the hospital was a black hole in her memory. There were a series of operations, impressions were made after her teeth had been cut out of her gums. False teeth would soon be inserted into her mouth and she would have to adjust to them. Her nose was righted and she could breath easier now. The chin and cheekbones had been restored. Her leg and arm didn't hurt as much now but were still in casts.

After months of laying in that awful bed, April was finally given a mirror and viewed herself for the first time. The shock was great. The face staring back at her was the face of a stranger. Jason had insisted that a beautician come in and help arrange her hair and assist her with makeup. After she had been made presentable, there was a big box of exquisite negligees from which to choose. April had never seen such beautiful lingerie in her life. With assistance, she was sitting in a chair when Jason entered the room. In his arms was a floral box containing beautiful yellow roses. The room already looked like a florist, she thought.

Seeing April sitting in the chair, he laid the roses on the bed and walked over to her. Handing her one, he kissed her hand and forehead. "Darling, you look so beautiful. God, I can't wait until I get you home. I have been so lonesome without you."

Taking both hands, he looked April straight into her eyes and said softly, "Darling, I know we were having a difficult time a short while ago, but since the accident I know I do not want to live without you. I love you with all my heart."

Before April could speak, Jason reached down and patted her stomach and said, "How's my little fellow today?"

"Senator", began April. "Please sit down, I have something important to tell you."

"Darling, the doctor said you were not to do too much talking right now. When I take you home, I'll take some leave and we'll spend a month talking and catching up on our lovemaking. That is, if the doctor says it's okay. Oh Betty, when I thought I had lost you, I didn't want to go on. You are my life."

Not knowing what to say, April sat back and looked at Jason Stewart. He was truly everything Betty had described him to be. Handsome, gentle and obviously deeply in love with his wife. What would he do when he found out that Betty was not the person in this room. Had she even survived? If so, where was she now?

"Senator," said April. "What happened to the girl in the seat next to mine?"

Jason cleared his throat and said softly, "She didn't make it darling, but you did. I don't know who she was or where she was coming from, but I thank God every minute that you were spared. The window of the plane was thrust out of the frame and a piece of metal went through her heart and lungs. She couldn't have known what hit her. I know its selfish but I am so thankful you didn't get your usual widow seat."

Standing up, Jason said, "The doctor told me not to stay too long. Since I want you home as soon as possible, why don't you let me help you back in bed and then I will disappear until tonight. If your are a good girl, I will arrange for the two of us to have a private dinner and wean you off hospital food." This was said with a boyish wink.

April was tired and the news about Betty greatly upset her. As Jason lifted her from the chair, she felt a tremor pass through her body. He encased her in his arms and held her close to his body. She smelled his scent and cologne. Before he left, he reached down and fondled one of her breast. Tears came to April's eyes. Seeing this, Jason kissed her firmly and hungrily on the lips. Softly he said, "It won't be long now and I'll have you home again. God I love you woman."

Saying this, he turned and walked to the door. Turning back, he blew a kiss to April. When he was no longer visible, April sobbed loudly, "Oh God, what am I to do?"

April began to assess her situation. She was in a hospital bed posing as a Senator's wife. She had a new face and was carrying another man's child. So far, it had only been a case of mistaken identity. Why oh why had Betty insisted on switching seats on the plane. "Oh God," moaned April, "What am I going to do?" How far was she going to allow this charade to continue? Needless to say, she was relieved when the nurse came in and gave her some medication that helped her to sleep. She didn't have to think when she was asleep. Yet she found herself remembering Jason's tenderness, his smell, and the passionate kiss. Had she really responded so willingly?

4

ARRIVING HOME

Getting out of the hospital was a blessing, but April was frightened. Could she pull this off? She had done a lot of soul searching in the hospital and decided that the only real option to protect her baby was to follow through the charade caused by the plane crash. The Senator needed a wife, she needed a home and her baby needed a father. Jason had been so kind and dedicated to her while she was recuperating, she knew in her heart she could easily share a life with him. In time, maybe love him.

The ride through the streets of Washington was breathtaking. She realized that she should not act like a tourist but it wasn't easy to avoid the beauty of the monuments and feel the electricity of this powerful city.

In a few months, April was to return to the hospital to correct some scar tissue caused by the plastic surgery. She was never less frightened than when she looked into mirror and saw Betty Stewart's face staring back at her. The hospital stay had been long and extremely painful. Regardless of her fate, she was glad to be outside again. Also, with makeup, she was able to conceal the rough areas.

An obstetrician had been recommended by the hospital and she was able to make an appointment as soon as possible. If movement was any indication of life, this little five month fetus was not giving an inch. It was determined to survive all odds. Just like its stubborn father, she thought.

A mental picture of Max appeared in front of her eyes and she felt tears well up inside her again. With all her might she banished this image and took a tighter hold of Jason's arm. Being the dutiful and kind person he was, he leaned over and kissed April on the cheek.

"Darling, it will be so good to have you home again. Daisy has been working like a slave preparing all your special dishes. The house is so clean I feel like an intruder. I was afraid to even blow my nose." They both laughed at that.

The trip took them through Georgetown. April had never liked close places and Georgetown was a mass of humanity and traffic. People literally pressed against the limousine and walked right in front of the cars. Jason felt the tension in her hand. "Baby, you will be okay. Guess one never gets used to the upbeat crowds that seem to be drawn to this area. We'll be home shortly and you can rest. But, only after you have one of Daisy's meals."

Shortly the limo slowed and made a left turn into a driveway. One would surely have to know this house was here thought April.

Jason helped April out of the car. The doctor had removed the hard cast and put her into a walking cast. As soon as she was out of the limo, a large black woman came running out of the house and literally consumed April with her arms. "Well, bless my stars, don't you look jist fine," she said. "You don't know how much a worry you done took from old Daisy's shoulders by coming home to this half crazed husband of yours. He don't eat, he don't sleep, he jist spends most of his days at the office and nights at the hospital. Jist look at him, ain't he a sight?"

"Daisy, please," said Jason.

"Lawd, I know, don't start wearing this pretty little thing out on her first day home. You jist come along with old Daisy honey, and we'll get you settled in your room. Senator, you sees that them bags get brought up."

April thought Daisy telling Jason what to do was comical and stifled a chuckle. Daisy, still with her arms wrapped around April proceeded to guide her upstairs.

"Lawd Miss Betty, I thought that man was gonna lose his mind when you got hurt. He stayed at the airport all night and even pitched in to help clear out that wreckage lookin for you. He knew what seat you was in and when they cut that section of the plane open, he was like a wild man. He run past the security, the firemen and everybody. He ran into the flames and found your seat. After he unbuckled your body, he lifted you up and run back out. His clothes was on fire and his hands was burned from the seat belt buckle. He swears to this day he never felt nothin. There's a picture in the paper showing the Senator holding your mangled body with tears runnin down his face. They literally had to force him to let you go so they could get you to the hospital. The doctors made him go home. Me and John, the chauffeur put him to bed and made sure nobody got through to him. He slept one hour, took a shower and got up and went back to the hospital. They had a time convincing him to have his burns treated. He still didn't feel nothin. He sent John back home and said if anybody needed him, call the hospital. That stubborn man refused to come home."

"Me and John tried to tell him you was too busy fighting for your life to worry bout him. He needed to get rested and be there for you when you got your strength back."

"Do you think he listened? Huh! He jist got in his car and drove to the hospital. John went down several times and took him some food and clean clothes. Otherwise, I hate to think what kind of a picture he would have made roaming them halls and pesterin them doctors bout your condition."

April was weary but glad Daisy was a conversationalist. She had learned a lot about her new "husband" in these first few minutes than she could have known in months. Daisy had been a nanny to Jason and when he came to Washington, she came with him. Her face was full of concern for her as well as for Jason. Betty must have been a favorite of hers too, she thought.

The pains of guilt were tearing at April's conscience. Jason had really loved his wife. What a shame, she thought. Her short introduction to Betty was one of an over indulgent, spoiled and selfish woman who loved her booze.

After April had been made comfortable, Daisy disappeared and Jason entered the room. "I should have warned you that Daisy has been crazy with concern. She probably will baby you for a while just to welcome you back home. When she found out about the baby, she went into orbit. My little boy is gonna be a daddy," she said. "I jist can't believe it."

Jason put his arms around April and said, "Darling, I hope you are feeling well enough to be home. I know that I'm sure glad you're here. The minute you walked through that door, the warmth of this house returned. Guess I never realized how much I missed you before. God woman but I love you." April yielded to his embrace and they kissed long and hard. Loving him was going to be the least of April's problems.

"Damn," he said. "I think we had better get you an appointment with that doctor soon and see what he says about sex. I'm not too sure how much longer I can wait to lay beside you and hold you again. I never knew how much I needed you until I thought I had lost you."

The embrace was broken only because of Daisy's reentry. She had brought cups of coffee and some delicious homemade cookies. Jason was right, April thought. Daisy was prepared to spoil her silly now that she was home.

April didn't drink coffee and felt awkward when she asked Daisy if she could please have a lemonade. After all, caffeine is not good for the fetus. Daisy just smiled and said it would only take a minute. Jason poured his coffee and ate a cookie. A few minutes later Daisy returned with the lemonade.

She also brought a tray of mail. "Most of it is get well cards, and there's a few invitations to society functions," said Daisy. April had to smile. So Daisy checks the mail too, she thought. This woman must truly hold a special place in this family with all the liberties she was taking. It was obvious that Jason would always be her little boy and would never outgrow his loving nanny.

Jason set his cup of coffee on the night stand and sat down on the bed. He started going through the mail with April. "Here's an invitation to the Congressional wives luncheon. I sure hope you feel well enough to attend that darling. John can drive you and bring you home. It's the end of this week and being held at the White House. This is a very important function for me politically. However, if you don't think you will be up to it, I will send regrets."

April just smiled back and said, "I would be proud to attend as Senator Jason Stewart's wife. If it helps you politically, I will do whatever I can." She prayed he and Daisy wouldn't hear the terror in her voice. How on earth could she pull this off. Oh God, she thought, what have I gotten myself into?

"Very good," said Jason. He was surprised as he remembered how Betty usually hated social functions and never wanted to engage herself in his affairs as a rule. He was pleasantly surprised and tried not to show it. He had prepared himself for her refusing to attend the function. Maybe this marriage will work after all, he thought. She certainly had been more affectionate since the accident. Oh well, he had heard that pregnancy affects women differently. Somehow he always thought Betty would resent being pregnant. They had had many discussions on the subject and she always made excuses about the time not being right. For now, he was happy, she was happy, don't try to fix something that ain't broke, his daddy always said.

They continued sorting the mail and decided on which ones to accept and decline. April stated that she would send regrets. The shock on Jason's face was real. Somehow, she knew she had made a blunder. Quickly, Jason said, "Darling that would be wonderful, but if you don't feel up to it, my secretary will be glad to take care of the replies."

April quickly stated, 'Whatever you think is best Jason is fine with me."

Daisy sensed the tension building. "Senator, you gotta let this pretty little thing get her rest. Now why don't you get on down to that office of yours while I takes care of Missy and cooks you a welcome home dinner you won't be forgetting for some time. Lord, you ain't nothing but skin and bones chile, and carrying a baby too. Well now that you're home ole daisy gonna make sure we put some color in them cheeks and some meat on them bones."

Jason checked his watch and quickly gulped down the rest of his coffee. "How on earth I ever got to be a U. S. Senator I'll never know. I can't even rule my own house. However, Daisy is right, as usual." Saying this, he winked at April. "There are things I need to take care of at the office and I will return at eight o'clock for that special dinner and dine with the most beautiful woman in the world." He got up and kissed April long and hard. Daisy just smiled. It was good to see these two so happy again. It had been rough before Betty left for Denver. Neither she nor Jason thought she would be back.

Daisy went to the closet and pulled out a dress that had a full skirt then looked back at April. "Don't know what you gonna wear to dinner. Your being pregnant and all. Staying in that hospital all the time, you ain't had no time to pick out no maternity clothes. Maybe this pretty dress with a stretch waistline will do. Listen chile, if you'd like, I'll have John drive me down to Woodies or Hechts and pick you out something suitable. With all them charges the Senator has set up for you, you could probably pick up the phone and have somethin delivered before eight o'clock."

April desperately wanted some time to herself. Things were happening too fast. Also, she needed to know where the dining room was. Seeing the opening, she turned to Daisy and said, "Daisy, I think that's an excellent idea. It's so sweet of you to offer."

Daisy was happy to run the errand, but only after she had extracted a promise from April that she would go to bed and not leave it until she returned. April smiled, reached over and hugged Daisy and told her that she was tired and would welcome the rest.

The minute she heard the car leave, April hobbled through the house. She walked through the upstairs opening door after door. One big shock was discovering that the Senator obviously had a bedroom to himself. Maybe their problems were more serious than April had first thought. This charade was not going to be easy.

There were several more bedrooms and bathrooms. Everything in the house was done in antiques. April had never liked heavy dark furniture and felt and oppression as she walked through the house. Some were obviously priceless, but still the house was so somber.

The stairs were not as easy to take as when Daisy was there to assist. However April managed to safely reach the bottom floor. Walking outside onto the patio, she saw that there was a guest house that sat back from the main house. Maybe Daisy lives there, she thought. Curtains over the garage implied that John also lived on he premises. Well, I'll find out soon enough, she thought, and reentered the house.

Returning to the bedroom April lay down and promptly fell asleep. The "tour" had tired her more than she thought. This is how Daisy found her when she returned from the shopping spree. Poor little thing, she thought, been through enough to put a healthy person to a test, let alone a pregnant one. Well now that she was home, Daisy could dedicate her life to making sure she had the best of care. That baby had to be healthy. The Senator's little boy, she thought. My baby's gonna have a baby. Shaking her head, she gently tiptoed out of the room.

Jason had warned Daisy and John that because of the trauma of the crash that Betty might have memory lapses. They were to try and ignore these episodes and assist her anyway they can.

Around seven o'clock Daisy entered the bedroom and gently shook April awake. 'I done run your bath honey and when you is done, ring the cord and I'll be back and help you get dressed. Hopefully that cast on your arm is going to come off soon. I sure do hope you like the dresses I brought home for you. If you don't we'll jist take them back tomorrow. Right now though, we gotta get you looking pretty for the Senator. He needs his home life to return to normal. That boy's been through a lot lately, worrying bout you and that baby. The first week you was in the hospital, I truly thought he was gonna lose his mind. After three days of settin beside your bed, we finally convinced him to come home and rest. The doctors promised to call if you woke up while he was home. Tonight, maybe he will eat and sleep like a human being.

April walked into the bedroom and crawled into the tub. Daisy had added some softeners and perfume salts. The water was just the right temperature. It was hard not to lay back and lounge in this atmosphere for an hour or more. Choosing not to upset Daisy, April got out of the tub and dried off. She walked into the bedroom and saw that Daisy had lain out several very pretty and very expensive maternity outfits. April looked at herself in the full-length mirror. She did have a protruding stomach, just enough she thought, to make every decent dress uncomfortable. She chose the pretty green chiffon dress that had a large lace collar that formed a V in the front. This would look good with her blond hair and green eyes. It felt good to wear normal clothes, even if they were maternity. There had been enough hospital wear to last her a lifetime. Even though the choices Jason had brought to the hospital were beautiful, it was boring to sit day after day dressed for bed.

April had just brushed her hair and finished applying lipstick when Jason entered the room. He came over to the dressing table and gave her a kiss. "Sorry I am late darling, but traffic was unbelievable. If your want to go down, I'll just change my shirt and jacket and meet you in the study." April was glad she had had an opportunity to tour the house earlier. Just as she descended the stairs, Daisy was entering a room with a tray of drinks. April followed. "Thought maybe you and the Senator would like a cocktail before dinner," she said.

"Thank you Daisy," said April. "You are so kind and considerate, I don't know what we would do without you."

Daisy just smiled and mumbled something about checking on dinner. Jason entered the study and picked up his drink. Handing one to April, he said, "Here's to the future. Your, mine and our son's"

"Jason, you won't be upset if its a girl, will you," asked April?

"Darling of course not, but I know its a boy. We are going to have a son."

April did not drink the cocktail but pretended to sip in honor of the toast.

She felt a pain in her heart every time Jason mentioned the baby. Putting her glass down she turned to Jason and said. "Please don't be angry with me, but I really don't think alcohol is good for the baby. Do you think there might be a soft drink in the house?"

Jason couldn't believe his ears. His hand shook but he hurriedly covered it up. Betty refusing a drink, what a miracle. So many times she had embarrassed him by drinking too much. God only knows how much she drank at home alone. If Daisy kept track, she never told Jason. When he had fully recovered he said, in as natural a voice as he could. "Of course dear, how callous of me." He hoped the happiness banging away in his heart wouldn't give him away.

Daisy appeared and stated that dinner was ready. What a dinner it was! She had truly outdone herself. There were fresh peas, mashed potatoes, a pot roast done to perfection with baby carrots, a salad with Daisy's own special dressing and homemade rolls. For dessert there was a Georgia peach cobbler. April and Jason both ate too much. A coffee for Jason and a ginger ale for April was served in the study. They relaxed and watched television for a while. Despite the afternoon nap, April was again tired. She was trying to stay awake just to spend time getting to know Jason. However when she looked over, Jason was nodding in his chair. April shook him gently and said, "Darling why don't we go upstairs to bed. You are so tired."

He stood up and draped one arm over April's shoulder and they walked up the stairs together. When they got to the top, he walked her to her bedroom and reached down and kissed her. April was taken back when he walked down the hall to his own room. She had forgotten that he slept alone. Why, she thought, if they loved each other so much, had this arrangement come about?

She entered her room, undressed, put on a flimsy negligee, brushed out her hair and walked through the adjoining door to Jason's bedroom. He was already undressed and in bed. April walked too the left side and slid in beside him. Jason was startled. "'Is something wrong darling," he asked?

"No," said April. "I just didn't want to be alone tonight, my first night back home. Jason, please make love to me and don't send me back to my room to sleep alone."

She was petrified, but if he was to be her husband, this had to happen soon. Why not now?

Jason was startled but gently and tenderly he removed her negligee and ran his hands over her swollen breasts and stomach. Never could he remember Betty responding so willingly and lovingly to each caress. This was the first time Jason recalled Betty's absolute surrender to passion. Their love life had been rather monotonous and routine. Her kisses were so passionate and he felt her desire.

Falling asleep from total and physical fulfillment, Jason's love for his wife was even greater than he ever believed it could be. Maybe, he thought as he curled her in his arms, we can get on with our lives. She had been so difficult those past few months prior to flying home. Whatever it took, he vowed, I am willing to do to keep her the way she is now. Kissing her again, he felt as if he would never be able to let go of her warm willing body.

April was surprised at how skillful and artful a lover Jason had been. She had always been told that southern men were great suitors outwardly, but lousy in bed. With a smile on her face, she fell asleep knowing that this myth was untrue. Jason was great in and out of bed. If this had been this good while she was pregnant, she couldn't wait until after the baby was born.

5

THE CONGRESSIONAL WIVES' TEA

John dropped April off at the White House for the tea. Even if she hadn't been here before, there was no chance of straying anywhere the secret service men didn't want you to go. She was escorted into the blue room and announced. Several women came over to April and said how happy they were to see her up and around. Congratulations on her pregnancy and how fortunate she was not to have lost it. One woman even told her that her husband said that Jason had been floating down the corridors of the Senate building since he discovered he was going to be a father. April smiled and try to make the right responses. Her heart was pounding and her knees were knocking loudly.

The blood drained from her face when she heard the next announcement. Mrs. Serena Hartley, wife of Congressman Hartley from Missouri. So Max had won the election after all.

Serena stood in the doorway looking even more beautiful than April remembered. She was obviously pregnant, but with her beauty, who would notice?

The punch in April's hand sloshed onto her dress. Hurriedly she sough a place to set the cup before she dropped it on the beautiful rug. A butler trained to sense problems, walked over with a silver tray and took the cup from April. She thanked him politely.

There was a protocol about sitting before the hostess arrives, so April walked behind some chairs and leaned against them. She prayed that her face would not betray her and her feelings. Serena could not know her. She was now Betty Stewart and had Betty Stewart's face. But, thanks to Max, she and Serena both had protruding stomachs.

Nothing could have prepared her for this meeting. Even if Jason had been at her side, she would not have been spared her reaction to Serena's presence.

When Serena had been introduced and approached April, she prayed that her knees would hold her. Somehow, through a fog of sheer self will, April said hello and shook Serena's hand. Thank god she wasn't at the end of the line and had to endure her presence for a longer period of time.

Everything that happened after that was a blur in April's memory. She could only hope and pray that she had said and done the right things. Time seemed to stand still for her. Why hadn't John come to take her home? Such was her thoughts when the first lady entered the room. With her presence, all the ladies were escorted into another room that had been set up with intimate little tables for welcoming speeches and a light lunch.

"I must get through this somehow," April said to herself. "I owe Jason that much. Since I chose this charade, I must endure whatever it takes to protect him herein. The press would have a field day if they ever found out that she had taken Betty Stewart's place; and she still had her baby to protect."

Fortunately, an older senators wife from Arizona came to her rescue. "Betty you look pale dear. Are you sure you are up to this luncheon or would you like to lie down? You've only been out of the hospital for a week. My chauffeur can run you home or if you wish, I'll be glad to sit with you if you wish to rest for a while."

Turning to the woman who was speaking, Betty put her hand on the woman's arm. "Thank you for being so considerate, I am tired, but I'm determined to see this through. This is the first function I have attended since the accident and I guess I'm just a little overwhelmed."

"That happens to me every time I attend one of these luncheons. My husband says, Mary, you attack those invitations like a hungry bear raiding a honey tree. Thank God you enjoy them. Course, if I ever get tired of attending social functions promoting his position, its time for us both to retire."

"That's a wise philosophy. It will do me well to remember it," said April.

With luck, Mary was seated at the same table as April and easily led the conservation. There was some talk about the riots in the north and south and fear was expressed about an overall confrontation. Laws had recently been introduced into the Senate and House concerning integration and bussing. Everyone agreed that written laws in the Legislative Branches had to be passed and enforced.

Conversations were interrupted by the welcome speech given by the First Lady. She encouraged each lady present to give full support to their husbands in all their endeavors. She also introduced all the new wives. There was a gentle suggestion made about how each lady and their families were now living in goldfish bowl. The press loved to flash headlines about the least bit of gossip. Therefore it was wise to be discrete as possible and try to let only one member of the family have all the attention; their husbands. Support was offered to the group if they ever encountered the wrath of the press. She ended with a reminder that a wife's conduct could make or break a politician's career. April felt a shudder when she thought what harm her deception could do to Jason. She must do everything in her power to continue until the end.

The luncheon was light. There was a delicious fresh salad and finger sandwiches. April did the best she could with the casted hand. Thank God it would be removed soon. Promptly at three o'clock, the First Lady left the dining room, signaling the party was over.

April was relieved. She was never so glad to get away from anything in her whole life. Yet some of the relief was from the fact that she had been readily accepted as Betty Stewart. She had passed the second test. The first was Jason. Yet somewhere in the back of her mind, the real challenge would be confronting Max. If seeing Serena could throw her into such a panic, she hated to think what reaction she would have around Max. She would always be linked to him because of the child she carried. "Dear God," she prayed. "Let me be worthy of this wonderful man who thinks I am his wife. Let me serve him justly and honestly. Lord make me worthy. Please make me worthy."

Daisy was hovering outside waiting for April to return. She saw how ashen she looked and immediately started protecting her and tried to usher her upstairs. April had had enough of her bedroom for a while and instead insisted on accompanying Daisy into the kitchen. She was unaware of Daisy's expression. Betty had only come into the kitchen approximately three times since they moved into this house.

Sitting at the table, April asked Daisy to pour her a glass of milk. Getting this, she asked Daisy to sit with her and fill in some of the missing gaps. Daisy was more than willing to assist. She began by saying "Chile you know all you have to do is jist ask ole Daisy anythin you wants to know. If I can help you in anyway, you jist let me know."

"Why all this oppressive furniture for such a beautiful house? Since I returned from the hospital I feel smothered by all this dark, old antiquated furniture all over the place."

Daisy threw her head back and laughed. "boy Miss Betty that sure must have been one big memory lapse, yes sir, hee hee. Dark oppressive stuff indeed."

April wondered if she had overstepped her boundary by this question, but she ached to know why Jason and Betty would fill such a small light and airy house with the "junk" that seemed to bust the seams wide open. The house could be so beautiful if only it was allowed to breathe.

"Miss Betty, that stuff has caused you and the Senator more trouble than a bad mother-in-law. Course it was his mother that wanted you to have all this stuff. When she was put into a nursing home, she agreed to go only if her "stuff" was taken care of. The Senator done said it cost him two months pay to have this junk hauled up here to Washington and what a pity it couldn't have gone to some museum or to a private collector. To keep the peace, he told his mom that you and him would guard each piece with your lives. Bless your souls, you have too."

"Some of the pieces in this house could be sold for enough money to feed half the state of Georgia. That is, if you could find some rich fool willing to buy it." Daisy laughed again. "Yes sir, they always said one man's junk is another man's treasure. Well this house if full of junk, a rich man's junk. Her daddy had the furniture market for years and always kept the choice pieces for himself. Naturally they got passed down. Only problem is, Jason never wanted them. Bein as he is a good and loyal son, he done what was expected of him for his mama."

April continued. "Daisy what if I told you I wanted to buy a house out of Georgetown?"

"Miss Betty, you done expressed again what you first said when you saw this house. The Senator got a good price on this place through a recommendation from a good friend in the realty business. Reckon you ain't changed your mind 'bout wanting to leave Georgetown. I remember your first year here. Couldn't hardly get you to leave the house you was so afraid. No, honey, you ain't got no memory lapse, what you is rememberin is absolutely correct. You ain't never liked this place. The house is overstuffed, jist like the crowd that mills around here all the time."

"Daisy, is John tied up all day every day with Jason or would he be free to take me around sometime?"

"Baby, all you gotta do is ask. The Senator can drive hisself to work or take a taxi. If you wants to use the limo, you jist say when. John will do anything you ask him to do. Specially if I tell him to." They both laughed at this.

"Daisy you have been such a big help to me. The rest of the week I'm going house hunting. Please find me the name of that agent so I don't make the same mistake twice. I want a house that is full of sun and light. A house you can entertain in and raise children without fear of putting permanent scars on expensive irreplaceable old furniture. I want a real home," said April.

"Miss Betty you know there is that dinner party at Senator Walker's house tomorrow night. Maybe you better get some rest before the Senator comes home tonight. I ordered more dresses for you and they come today. Also, Rene' called bout your hair appointment at four. You might want me to make it earlier in case you wants to get your nails done too. Anyway, you lets me know. I'll take care of it for you. Now I've gotta get back to my dinner. You and Jason looking good after eatin ole Daisy's cooking. Got some color back in your cheeks. If you need anything you jist call, I'll be right here in the kitchen."

April walked out to the patio. She laid in one of the chaise lounges that had been set out of the sun. The dinner party frightened her. If Jason had accepted for them, she knew it was important. With him on her arm, she knew it would be easier, but she was afraid. It wasn't her physical self she was fighting, it was her mental self. She must have been out of her mind thinking she could continue this charade. Just then the baby decided to have a kicking exercise and she was reminded again of why she had made the choice she did. Hurriedly, she walked past Daisy to the stairs. She was so afraid of seeing Serena and Max. Would they be there? Could she handle seeing them? It had to happen, there was no way she could avoid him forever. The political circle was too small.

Sitting in the bedroom, April had found old photo albums and was savoring the past she couldn't have known with Jason. He was a handsome little boy, an only child of elderly parents. His father had died of cancer and his mother had broken her hip last year and had been put in a fine rest home. It had bothered Jason to put her there, because he was so dedicated to doing the right and proper thing. According to Daisy, the old woman compromised only after Betty and Jason agreed to take good care of her "stuff".

There were pictures of Betty in her wedding gown and many photos of her and Jason in casual attire at different functions. Betty didn't smile as much as April thought she should have though. It was as if she was holding something back. That she held some mysterious secret that the world would never know. Whatever it was, pondered April, she took it to the grave with her. Maybe she was unhappy way back then.

Because of the foresight of someone in the past, there were dates in the albums and on the backs of the pictures. Because of this, she was able to determine their wedding date, and hers and Jason's birthdays.

She was so engrossed in the albums that she didn't hear Jason enter the bedroom. He walked up behind her and kissed her hair. Feeling secure only when he was around, April sprang up from the chair and put her arms around his neck. They kissed long and hard.

"Now that's how a man's supposed to be welcomed after a long hard day's work," he said. Releasing her, he began to loosen his tie and remove his shoes. "How was the luncheon?"

April replied that it was a very nice affair. That all the wives were sympathetic to her and offered support to each other. She especially enjoyed seeing Mary. Hopefully, Jason would know who Mary was, she thought. She went on to describe the food and the speech the First Lady made.

Jason listened intently. What he was thinking was concealed behind a smile. Usually when Betty went to these affairs, she would come home drunk and he would find her passed out. She did enjoy her booze.

They discussed the dinner party at the Walker's. April tried casually to find out who might be there.

Jason had been casual in answering by saying the usual crowd and perhaps a few new faces. This set April's heart pounding. "Dear God," she prayed silently, "please don't let Serena and Max be part of the new faces."

After kissing her again, Jason undressed and stepped into the shower. He had a fine body. Long legs, thin hips and waist. Just seeing him naked made her anticipate bedtime. Inwardly she chided herself. Was she a nympho who couldn't get enough of her "husband?" She never knew that sex could be so good. Her mind let her think about what it would be after the baby was born. That was worth sticking around for. If only she could keep her secret. Her life was dedicated to trying.

While Jason was dressing, she slipped into her bedroom and put on the dress Daisy had arranged for her. On an impulse, she put her hair up and slid some beautiful silver combs in it to hold it in place. She had just finished her makeup when Jason appeared in the doorway. He had changed and looked more handsome than prince charming.

"Excuse me lady," he said. "Didn't we have a dinner date tonight?" April giggled. He continued. "Would Mrs. Stewart allow me to escort her to a table for two downstairs?"

She got up from the dressing table and took his arm. Together they walked down the staircase and into the dining room. Again Daisy had put together a feast. They ate, they talked and flirted with each other. Both were anxious to end the meal and get up to the bedroom. Yet they owed it to Daisy and her efforts to take full advantage of her delights. Somehow they endured their urges through dessert.

Their passion were peaked by the time they were both undressed. Their sex was getting better and better. Jason said he felt like a teenager. This he said while holding April close and nibbling on her ear. She admitted that she loved the way he brought her to her peak by touching sensitive areas. If he was shocked, he didn't show it. They lay together all night, interrupted only by April's call to the bathroom. Seems half her time each day was running back and forth to the potty.

Jason rose early, as he did each day and went down for breakfast. April joined him. If Daisy was surprised, she didn't show it. Usually Betty didn't get up until after ten o'clock and then she wanted a tray in the bedroom. She liked what she saw. Betty had positively bloomed from pregnancy. She was a more likeable person and was obviously in love with Jason again. Daisy was well aware that only one bed had to be made each morning and this was the best news.

April's hair appointment had been changed to two o'clock and this gave her additional time to have her makeup done professionally also. If she was going to be Jason's wife, she was damn well going to present the best picture she could.

When John drove her to the beauty shop, April was apprehensive. A woman could forget many things in life, but her hairdresser — never. Fortunately Rene' came to the limo and took her by the arm. "How is the beautiful Senator's wife today," he asked?

"Rene', how about we lighten the hair a bit and do something totally wicked with it for the Walker's party tonight?"

"Darling, I am your slave. I can give you a provocative hair style that will make you the envy of the whole town if you just say the word and trust me completely."

"Let's go for it," said April. "I need a change and this just might be it."

Hours later April emerged from the shop with a radiance she felt within her soul to the ends of her smile. No more just Betty Stewart. She wasn't going to hide what this gal had to offer, even pregnant. Look out Washington, she felt like singing, Betty Stewart is emerging! She was going to make sure that Jason took notice of her and be proud to present his "wife" to all his colleagues and their wives. April felt reborn.

When she arrived home Daisy couldn't hide her approval. "Lawdy mercy, wait till that man of yours sees what Rene' done to this woman tonight. He won't leave your side for one minute at that party, I jist bet. If we hurry we can get you dressed before he comes home and you can surprise him good," she said.

April liked what she saw in the mirror. The hair, the makeup, and the beautiful black crepe dress was total perfection. Jason would be surprised, she thought.

Surprised wasn't quite the word. He had April stand up and walk back and forth. "Daisy," he said, "do you suppose we brought the wrong woman home from the hospital? If we did, lets not tell anyone and keep her, okay!"

April tried not to show shock. At first she though that he had discovered her deception. Then she realized that Jason was teasing her. She forced a smile and kissed him on the lips. "Just try and return me," she said lightly as she could, praying that her voice wasn't betraying her.

Daisy jist stood beside April and smiled. She sure liked to see these young folks happy. Nothing had been said when she noticed that April wasn't sleeping in her bed at night. Ole Daisy knew all the secrets of the house and she was sure glad about this one. Something good was coming out of all that tragedy. This was going to be a good year for them all. She felt it in her bones.

Jason excused himself and returned shortly with one of the most exquisite necklaces April had ever seen. "Darling, this occasion seems so special, maybe you would like to wear these diamonds with that beautiful dress."

April almost fainted. Diamonds! Real diamonds being fastened around her neck.

She tried hard not to cry and ruin her makeup. Jason opened his hand and showed her the matching earrings. Then he disappeared into his bedroom to dress.

Daisy said "Chile, that necklace has been in the family for over a hundred years. I never seen that boy even so much as hint bout you wearin it. You really are special tonight. I wants you both to have an extra special good time."

April hugged Daisy. "Thank you for rearing such a wonderful sensitive and caring man. I'm sure we'll have a special good time."

Jaons was so attentive, even in the limo. Both were thinking about after the party. There was a magnetism between them tonight that words could not express. Even in her advanced pregnancy, their lovemaking was so wonderful, tender and fulfilling for both of them.

Daisy was right about his not leaving her side even for a minute. April found herself casting loving glances at him every chance she got. He really was a handsome and loving man. Surely she had made the right decision in the hospital to become Betty Stewart.

The Walker's lived in Bethesda and their house was magnificent. It was huge but so tastefully done that it gave an intimate appeal. April asked Carolyn who had done the decorating. She was surprised when Carolyn said that she did it herself. With Jack gone all day to the Senate and working late into the night, she hired a consultant and began creating an atmosphere best suited to her taste. It had been fun, but she admitted, she was glad when it was completed.

April expressed her desire to move out of Georgetown and find a similar, somewhat smaller house in this area. Carolyn was delighted and promised to call her and put her in contact with a reputable Realtor who would see that her dream house was located.

Everything had gone perfectly up to that point. However, just before dinner was called, Serena and Max appeared in the doorway. They made their way around the room making apologies for having taken a wrong turn and arriving late.

April took a deep breath when they headed her way, and clasp Jason's arm a little harder. She was transfixed by Max's face. Agony was replaced by relief when she realized that the pain was not as great as she had anticipated. She realized then and there that she loved Jason. Just when she had come to realize this, she did not know. Now that she had seen him, she could put her misplaced love and hate to rest concerning Max. Jason was her life. She would do whatever it took in the future to make him happy.

Looking up at Jason, she smiled sweetly and told him that she loved him dearly. She needed to say those words to him. He smiled and tightened his grip on her hand. Nothing was going to part them.

Max was seated on April's right and even this did not disturb her. Jason was on her left. Her rock, her lover, her kind and generous companion was there for her.

"You certainly look well after the encounter you experienced this summer," said Max.

"I feel fine. It took some lengthy hospital time, but with today's medicine they put me back together quite nicely. I still have more surgery after the baby comes though. There's still some scar tissue that has to be removed. Minor though, compared to what I have already been through," said April.

"Serena and I attended the funeral for April Simmons, a dear friend of mine who wasn't so fortunate. She was a wonderful, sweet, and intelligent girl. Also a friend and confidant who was invaluable to me and my campaign. It is hard realizing that she is gone. We grew up together, you know."

With a smile on her face, April hoped her true feelings were hidden. "You bet your sweet ass I know. If I was so valuable, whatever made you turn from me to Serena. If you hadn't been such a bastard, I wouldn't have been on that plane."

For the rest of the meal, April turned her attention to Jason and the guests across the table from her. She had had quite enough of Max Hartley for one night. Strange, she thought, they are both so shallow they deserve each other.

After dinner drinks were served and guests strolled casually around the house and pool, April was unaware that everyone was whispering about how she had refused all alcohol during the meal and afterwards. Also, how beautiful she looked.

It was a beautiful night and April was in a romantic mood. She had faced down her major demon and felt comfortable. Somehow she sensed that Jason wanted to be alone with her too. They needed each other tonight badly and to hell with the rest of the world. This attitude kept her smiling and saying correct things to people introduced to her. She was actually glad that she was now able to put her life on the right track. She now knew she truly loved Jason. Thank God she had found out early in their relationship.

6

MAX HARTLEY

Max was excited when he discovered that he had won the election. Growing up poor, he learned early in life that hard work and perseverance were tools for rewards. His ambition for political life was fulfilled with this win. Soon he and Serena would be heading for Washington, D. C. Unfortunately, he soon discovered that the beautiful Serena who had dazzled him with her intelligent conversation and beauty, was a mere shell of a woman. She was selfish, cruel and had one ambition in life. That was to please her father. True Henry had been the force behind Max's win, but when Max had time to look back over the events during the campaign, he was amazed at how successfully he had been maneuvered through a short engagement and wedding. He had been so smitten with Serena's beauty and his greed for this chance for a future in the political world that he would have sold his soul. As it was, he had only lost the only woman he now knew that he would ever love. April was so kind and gentle. They had been in love for years and lovers only recently. Why, he kept asking himself, why did she have to get pregnant now. He couldn't afford a scandal at this point in his career. Hell, he didn't even have a career yet. He had only just won the election. When he heard that April had been killed in a plane crash he tried to hide his grief. Only she and he knew that he had also lost a child. God how he wished he could have been kinder to April. Her face, with the tears streaming down her cheeks, would always haunt him. She had been so radiant when she had told him the news about the baby. Truly she was not expecting his reaction to be rejection. Quietly she said that Max would never have to be embarrassed by her. Shortly afterwards, she disappeared from his life. It was only through the media that he found out that she had been aboard that fatal flight. Because of Serena's jealousy, he could not grieve openly.

She must never know about April, the only true love of his entire life.

Serena hadn't wanted to get married. Her father told her to, so she did. She hadn't wanted to get pregnant. Her father told her to, so she did. Truth be known she hated marriage, sex and Max. Also she hated being pregnant. How was she going to make a statement in Washington with a protruding stomach? She had envisioned herself chairing important committee's and making her father proud of her progress. Also it would help the junior status that Max held. If she could make herself well known and kept her face and views in the media, her father's prediction of Max's going all the way could become a reality.

Their move to Washington was a nightmare. Serena cried for days before the move. She hadn't realized that the move really meant that she had to leave her father. Henry told Max it was just her pregnancy that was causing her to act in this manner. His little girl was a professional. She would smile when it was expected, hang onto Max's arm, pose for pictures and say the right thing at the right time. She had class. Max was not to worry.

Serena hated Washington. The weather was nasty and her morning sickness morning, noon, and night didn't help much. Max was always away at work and delighted in telling her of his accomplishments at the end of the day. The only thing that kept her sane was shopping. At least there was excellent stores in the area. When she had their son, her father would give her the money from her trust fund and she could spend to her hearts delight. Max certainly didn't make enough money to keep her in the style she was accustomed to. He had even expected her to do all the household chores. Heaven forbid. They had to have domestic help. The apartment they had chosen was expensive and he had complained about that. Well, he might have been able to adjust to such accommodations but she certainly couldn't.

The Congressional Tea was a disaster. She had intended to make a fashion statement. The dress had cost a fortune and she knew that she had never looked better, in spite of her pregnancy. However, all the attention was given to Betty Stewart. It was unfortunate she had been in a severe accident but Serena had boned up on the latest issues and read everything in sight so she could talk intelligently at this luncheon. Yet, no matter what subject she approached, the conversation returned to Betty Stewart and how fortunate she was to have survived and how beautiful she looked. She left the tea hating Betty Stewart.

7

THE HOUSE

Carolyn was true to her word. She called April the following morning with the name of a Realtor. As they talked, it was agreed that they would meet around one o'clock and be driven through the Bethesda area in search of the right home. A limousine would call for Betty and the Realtor and then would drive out to pick up Carolyn.

Daisy was all a flutter. April had had a rough night after the dinner party. She and Jason had made love but April could not shake a feeling of total exhaustion. Well, it was summer and she was in her seventh month of pregnancy. Only when she promised to rest all morning did Daisy finally concede to her house hunting venture.

April was truly impressed with the houses chosen for her to view. There was a new area just opening with a few custom built homes called Potomac. This area was just off Rockville Pike and close to Bethesda.

The third house was exactly what April was looking for. The house was approximately ten years old and each room was large and spacious. Windows adorned every room bathing them in sunlight. Even the kitchen had a skylight. There were six bedrooms, a den and servants quarters. This house was designed for April. She and Carolyn accompanied the Realtor back to the Walker's home. April agreed to call the agent as soon as she discussed the sale with the Senator.

Carolyn asked Betty if she would like for her to assist in the decorating. She had plenty of time and she would be cheaper than an interior decorating firm.

April readily agreed. They sat over tea and discussed where the nursery would be, what colors the bedrooms should be done in; the den, the living room and even the foyer. However, she told Carolyn she wouldn't do anything about the kitchen until Daisy saw it. In fact, Daisy would be the deciding factor on the house. Her input was so invaluable to her and Jason.

April was so caught up in the magic of her dream that she completely lost track of time. Carolyn had her chauffeur drive her home.

Daisy was waiting on the steps. "Lawd honey I thought you was never coming home. Now you promised ole Daisy you wouldn't over do. Jist look at you. You are so tired and you been on your feet all day. Jist look at that swelling. I should never have let you out of the house today. If somethin happens to you, the Senator will have my hide."

All April could think about was getting upstairs and laying down. Daisy ranted and raved all the way up the stairs. It was so rewarding to have someone care for you as much as Daisy's guardian angel manner.

When Jason arrived home, April was still asleep. She had Daisy get her a heating pad as her back was hurting something awful. What April did not know was that Daisy had taken a chair by the window in her bedroom and sat quietly in watch over her. Daisy knew that April was in trouble but did not want to alarm her. She had already called the doctor.

Jason came up to the bedroom and Daisy motioned for him to be quiet. She joined him in his bedroom and told him that Betty had been looking at houses all day and she was exhausted. Also, her ankles were swollen out of her shoes. Daisy had seen a lot of pregnant women in her lifetime and this one had the look of one in deep trouble.

They both heard April moan at the same time. When they got into her bedroom they saw that she was struggling to get up. Daisy saw the blood and mucus. "Her water done broke," said Daisy. "Senator, you call an ambulance. Tell them to get here quick. This chile is gonna deliver anytime now. Tell the hospital to be on the alert for a preemie."

Jason did as he was instructed while Daisy sat with April and tried to calm her. It was only a few minutes until they heard the whaling of a siren. April was trying to be brave, but the pain was unbearable.

Jason rode with her in the ambulance. Daisy and John followed in the limo. Daisy prayed for April, the baby and that John's driving wouldn't get them both killed.

The doctor was waiting for them at the hospital. The trip was short. April was taken into emergency and Dr. Whittier stood waiting. He had her admitted and put her into a labor room and examined her. Jason filled out the form while April was placed in stirrups.

"Doctor," she said, "the pain is so intense."

"Just hold on, don't push. Let me have a look see and then we'll go from there," he said.

Dr. Whittier did not like what he saw. The baby was not in the proper position to be born. Its feet were in the birth canal. He told a nurse to stand by and he promptly left the room.

Quickly he explained to Jason that the baby was breech and he suggested he do a caesarean section immediately. Even with that, there might be complications. The baby was still premature.

Jason signed the forms and accompanied the doctor into the labor room.

"'Betty, darling, we are going to prepare you for a caesarean section. The baby is breech and there's too much chance involved for a normal deliver. They are going to prep you now and have you in surgery in about an hour. Can you hold on that long?"

April smiled and said, "You tell me, you're the Senator and he's the doctor."

Jason gave April a kiss and left the labor room. Before he did, he bent down and said, "Now we'll be a complete family, honey. You, me and little Jason Junior. I will be here throughout your delivery. Darling I love you and you are about to make me the happiest man alive. God woman, I love you." With this, he kissed her again and patted her hand.

April tried really hard not to cry. Oh God, why couldn't this baby be his. He is such a good man. Why oh why does life have to be so cruel?

The surgery was short and uneventful. April delivered a five pound baby boy. He was small, but loud. His head was covered with long black hair. Even without being cleaned up, he was beautiful. If anyone believes in clones though, this baby was definitely cloned from Max's genes. They baby was his miniature in every conceivable way.

Jason was beside himself when he saw the baby. "He is absolutely beautiful. I knew it would be a boy, I just knew it. Honey, can we call him junior or did you have some other name in mind?"

April was so flattered that Jason wanted to name his child junior. She said a silent prayer that Jason would never know that this child, this son that made him so happy, was not his own flesh and blood.

Looking into Jason's beautiful eyes, she smiled and said, "Jason Junior is a fine name."

No baby was more anxiously awaited by those who love him. Daisy was beside herself. When April and Jason took the baby home, Daisy just took over. If she could have breast fed him, she would have done that too. Daisy just wanted her family to be happy.

She not only babied April, but anticipated every breath little J. J. took. April feared that so much work would make Daisy ill. No way, Daisy insisted, this was a pure labor of love.

Several times April tried to persuade Daisy to let her obtain a nurse for the baby. Her watching him night and day was just too much for a woman her age.

Daisy would not hear of it. She had waited thirty eight years for this opportunity and she was going to enjoy it. She was holding her babies boy. Jason had a son.

April received a call from her "father" in Boulder. He said he would be flying to see her and the baby in a couple of weeks. This was his only grandchild and he had to rearrange his surgical calendar first. April was apprehensive at first, but everyone had been so kind. Surely she could fool her "father" too.

Jason had started coming home for lunch just to grab a sandwich and have a look at his heir. April vowed to have as many more children as he wanted. She desperately wanted to have his "real" child. If he could feel this way about a bastard, surely he could show the same sentiments for his own flesh and blood.

Carolyn came to visit and told April that when she was well enough, she wanted her to come to lunch. Bring the baby, she invited. Being a Senator's wife in Washington, D. C. often includes the sacrifice of leaving all one's family in the home state. Visits are never often enough or long enough. She anxiously wanted to cuddle a baby. When Jason and April asked the Walker's to be the godparents, they readily agreed. Little Jason would be baptized in the Foundry Methodist Church off of DuPont Circle when he was six weeks old. He was small, but his lungs were as strong as any normal full term baby. He had been in the house only an hour when everyone knew who was in charge.

Invitations had been on hold until April could get her strength back. Because elections were coming up soon, she wanted to be as visible with her husband as possible. Everyday she exercised and experimented with colors and new makeup to make herself more acceptable to the public. Soon they would be going home to Georgia where Jason would campaign. April had every intention of being an active member in his campaign.

It had been a hard day for all and the heat and humidity had caused little Jason to break out in a horrible heat rash. He was uncomfortable and made sure everyone around him shared his pain. Therefore, when April and Jason fell asleep that evening, it was understandable why they didn't hear the telephone until it had rung six or eight times.

Jason took the call and said, "Yes, this is Senator Stewart. What! Oh no."

April was instantly alerted to the tone in his voice. When Jason hung up he turned to her and put his arms around her. "Darling, I am so sorry. That was your father's partner in Boulder. Your dad had a fatal heart attack tonight at eight o'clock. He went suddenly."

April's reaction was one of shock. How could she not feel sorry about this event. Even if she didn't know this man, she had to continue the charade she had begun when she chose to become Jason's wife. She and Jason were instantly awake and began to make arrangements to fly April home for the disposition of the body and property. "This may sound selfish, but it couldn't have happened at a worse time for me," said Jason.

April realized that he was not being unkind, he just had a full schedule to complete prior to leaving for Georgia to campaign. Also, they had to work out arrangements with his mother to donate all the antiques to a historical society or one of the antebellum homes in Georgia in her name. April had come up with this scheme, hoping to appease both her mother-in-law and not tread on his loyalty or cause a family scene.

It was finally decided that April would travel to Boulder alone. It would be hard to leave a seven week old baby, but in Daisy's hands, she knew he would be well taken care of.

The apprehension of flying to a strange place where she was supposed to know everyone filled April with terror. Also, the fear of getting back on an airplane was not going to be easy. In the essence of time, these arrangements were made and April was obligated to take the next step into her strange and new future.

8

THE FUNERAL

The flight was uneventful, other than the butterflies in April's stomach. What am I to do when people expect me to recognize them, she thought. Well, she had come this far and could not back out now.

There was a car there and the man who approached April was obviously her "father's" partner. He asked if she would like to go home and freshen up first and then go to the funeral home and make arrangements, or wait until morning to finalize everything.

April was so weary that all she wanted was a bath and a quick nap. However, she insisted that they go by the funeral home and make the arrangements. Once done, she could get a good night's sleep and not worry about facing this task in the morning. This also meant she could return to Washington sooner.

As it turned out, there wasn't much to do. Dr. Sloane was a rock and made suggestions that April found reasonable and in excellent taste. He said that he would acquire the death certificate and arrange for the minister and church.

April really did not know how to thank this man for his kindness when he dropped her at home. He just shrugged and said he was glad to do it for his old friend.

Imagine April's surprise when she saw that the house had been taken over by relatives and well wishers. Food and flowers were everywhere.

Realizing that the flight was obviously stressful for her, they insisted that she rest. Before she could, though, she had to call Daisy and ask about J. J. She knew that Jason was tied up with a full appointment schedule today so she asked Daisy to give him her love and to let him know that she had arrived safely.

After a couple of hours of total deep and uninterrupted sleep, April ventured downstairs. There was a little old man sitting in her living room. He identified himself as a Realtor who asked if she thought it was callous if he represented her in selling the house. She said that in the interest of time, that might be a good ideal. There were prayers tonight so in the interim she listened to suggestions for disposition of family items. She asked if there was a church organization or perhaps a Salvation Army nearby that would take possession of the household furnishings. This was discussed with several people and they agreed to get back with her. All in all, things went really well.

After prayers and endless lines of people who shook hands and offered condolences, April went back to Betty's childhood home. Somehow, selfishly, she thanked God for protecting her identity. Now that Betty's father was regrettably dead, she had one less fear of being discovered.

Searching through the house, she found pictures of Betty when she was a baby right through to her wedding. Without realizing it, she had set up until early morning going through memorabilia. Betty seemed to have a very happy and eventful life. She had been popular in high school and college. There were enough pictures of her in this house to fill seventeen albums.

Feeling weary, April turned out the light and slept. Her thoughts were not with the man in the funeral home. There were with the man and child back in Washington. April could only thank Betty for exchanging seats with her on that fatal day when the airplane crashed. She felt pains of guilt, but her happiness of establishing such a wonderful future for herself overrode guilt. One thing that really bothered her was that Jason's real son had perished in the crash. He was raising Max Hartley's child and he, nor Max, must never know.

Around nine o'clock the next morning a well dressed man called on April. He introduced himself as a Mr. Adams from the Boulder First National Bank. He wished to inform her of her father's holdings and ask for instructions for disposition. He suggested that she accept a transfer of accounts to her bank in Washington. If she would be so kind as to give him this direction and power of attorney, it would be completed within a week. April was shocked. She had not had even the remotest thought about any inheritance. Recovering from this news, she thanked Mr. Adams and said that she would get in touch with him after she conferred with her husband.

She also had to discuss the partnership with Dr. Sloane. What insurance policies had been established, did it leave the practice to the surviving partner, or did it allow the survivor to purchase the deceased partner's interest?

This didn't take long to discover because the next visitor was the insurance agent who had been a boyhood friend of Betty's father. The partnership was dissolved upon the death of the other. This was a relief to April. She didn't know what she would have done otherwise. Also, there were several policies leaving her as the sole beneficiary. They amounted to well over a million dollars. As his practice progressed, Betty's father had taken steps to ensure that his daughter would be taken care of for life. This caused great guilt on April's part, but she thought about her son. If she was ever found out, this would assure her son a future.

The next person was truly a puzzle to April. An elderly woman approached her and apologized for calling about this matter during Betty's time of grief. However, she knew that Mrs. Stewart would be leaving for Washington soon and she felt this would be her only chance to speak to her. April had to admit that her curiosity was peaked.

The woman introduced herself as a Mrs. Baker who was involved with social services. She apologized again for being so forward, but there was no other way to approach the subject.

"Would you consider donating your father's house to the county for use by battered women and runaways?"

Before April could answer, Mrs. Baker continued.

"I realize the monetary value as well as the sentimental value, but there is a real need for a dwelling such as this in this area for women and children. They need a place where they could feel safe. Your father was very active in this cause and allowed several families to share his house while they were receiving counseling and cooling off. I know this comes at a bad time and the request is probably a shock, but I had to come by and talk to you before you returned to Washington."

"Properties are so expensive, this is a well built house in a nice neighborhood. To put it mildly, it's perfect. The location couldn't be better even if we had the funds to build a shelter. Your father probably broke the ground for this type of shelter as he was always working with and housing some of our overflow people. Mrs. Stewart, Betty, won't you at least consider this request?" asked Mrs. Baker.

April was truly impressed with this woman's sincerity and straight forwardness of her campaign speech. It took a lot of courage to approach anyone with a request of this nature.

April thanked Mrs. Baker for stopping by and said she would consult her father's lawyer and check out the legalities. She wasn't saying no. In fact, she wanted something left from Betty's heritage and this could be the mortality April could give her.

April excused herself when the telephone rang. Mrs. Baker said she would see herself out. Jason was on the telephone. He said he was flying in for the funeral, if she didn't think this would distract the funeral. Sometimes the presence of a U. S. Senator overwhelms people. April assured him that she would be thrilled to have him attend. Her heart soared. There were millions of questions about the baby and Daisy. The proud tone was still in Jason's voice. His chest had swelled to point of buying new shirts, she teased. April said that she couldn't wait to start working on a brother or sister for J. J. Jason was surprised, but said he would gladly do his part. Especially if they had another child like J.J.

When April hung up, she knew that she could get through anything now that Jason was going to be by her side. Again, she silently thanked God for the events that lead up to her good fortune.

The funeral was very tastefully done and it seemed as if the whole town of Boulder had elected to attend. With Jason beside her, the crowd was more reserve then if she had been alone. She appreciated this.

Jason and April continued back to the house to sign papers for the money transfer from the bank, the insurance forms, and a document giving Mrs. Baker the use of the house for battered women and runaway children. To this, Jason added their personal check for $25,000.00 to get the enterprise started. He explained in depth that this was a local problem and not one which could expect subsidies from the government.

April left word with Mrs. Baker that she would return yearly and help raise money for the enterprise, if her schedule would permit.

Packing up personal belongings was difficult. She followed Jason's lead as he certainly knew what Betty had treasured and would have wanted to keep. Mostly they took scrapbooks, books and dolls. Arrangements were made for clothing and other articles to be picked up by charitable organizations.

The plane ride was much more comfortable than the one taking her to Boulder. She sat back, eyes closed, hand in hand with the man she loved, and let her thoughts wander.

Jason, looking over, thought she was sleeping. Poor dear, he thought, she has had a rough time this year. Well, we have a lifetime together that will make her forget. I hope.

9

THE SURPRISE

The landing at National Airport was smooth, in spite of the storm. John was waiting in the limo. After collecting the baggage, they began the ride home. April's heart was pounding. She couldn't wait to see her baby.

Daisy was waiting on the steps with little J. J. in her arms. Each time April looked at her darling son she was amazed at seeing Max Hartley's face staring back at her. He was a handsome little baby, and she still feared that they would be found out. Jason only seemed to see what he chose to see, a son he had wanted and waited so long for. He worshiped this child.

After Jason and John had taken the bags inside, Jason asked if April, Daisy and J. J. were up to taking a little ride. He stated that he had made arrangements to take the rest of the day off. He loved to surprise April.

April didn't seem to think this was unusual. Jason had tried, especially since the baby arrived, to spend more and more time with his family. This more than made up for the nights he worked until the wee hours trying to formulate policy or muster votes for important bills.

Taking J. J. from April, Jason opened the limo door and said to Daisy, "My lovely damsels, won't you join me for a lovely ride in the country?"

Inside the limo Daisy and April talked about what the baby had done in April's absence. She had asked Daisy what he was eating, he had grown so much in a week's time. Before they knew it, the limo had stopped.

John stepped out and opened the car door. They were standing in front of the house that April had discussed buying with Carolyn.

"How do you like your new home, Mrs. Stewart," asked Jason.

April was dumbfounded. "Jason, you bought this house for me! Oh my wonderful darling. I love it! I just love it!"

Turning to Daisy, she asked, "Have you seen the kitchen? I told the Realtor I wouldn't even consider buying this beautiful house until Daisy gave her approval?"

Daisy laughed and said that she had indeed seen the kitchen.

Jason took the key from his pocket and opened the door. April could not believe her eyes. The house was completely furnished and it was beautiful.

"Jason how on earth did you do all this by yourself," asked April?

"Well now, I guess you are entitled to know my little secret. I called Carolyn and she agreed to start without you. Seems you had many conversations with her about how you would like this house to look. She has worked like an absolute love slave to make sure it would be ready for you when you got back from Denver. Now we can move in before we go to Georgia to campaign. We will come home to this beautiful house that you wanted to raise lots of babies in. I have now provided the space, so girl stand by. We have six bedrooms. Think we can fill them all?"

April was beside herself with joy. She had her house. Carolyn was going to continue to help her decorate. It was going to be a glorious year.

On the ride back home Jason mentioned that Congressman Hartley's wife had a baby girl. She was due to come home from the hospital tomorrow. This information did not bother April as much as she thought it would.

Jason mentioned several causes that April might want to be involved in. However, both decided to wait until after the election and the move into the new house. Enough was enough at this point.

The next few weeks was spent in going through Betty's closet to assure that she had proper clothes for April to wear while campaigning. Fortunately they wore the same size. Betty had excellent taste, but everything was so tailored, bordering on severe. April liked ruffles and frills. She tried not to be too extravagant in her shopping though. She did not want the public to think that clothes were her only interest. Also, Jason needed the poor man's vote as well as the rich man's to return to the Senate.

It was finally time to travel to Georgia and both Jason and April had full schedules. He was clearly surprised when he mentioned several functions that he could not attend, April said she would be happy to fill in for him. Betty had never shown any interest in his campaigning, and only attended social functions that Jason insisted were important to his career.

April went over several speeches she had written on Jason's behalf and got his approval before they went their separate ways on the campaign trail. She intended to campaign just as hard as he did. It was the least she could do for this wonderful man. Her experience gained in helping Max get elected to Congress was extremely helpful to her. She had forgotten how interesting political campaigns could be.

10

THE CAMPAIGN

April had occasion to meet Jason's mother. Fortunately the woman only had few coherent moments. She had recently turned seventy nine years old and lived mostly in the past. She was forty when she had Jason. When April thought Mrs. Stewart was lucid, she mentioned all the gorgeous antiques being donated in her name to the Georgia Historical Society to be used in the beautiful antebellum homes on display throughout the state. After a few moments, the old woman agreed that this was an excellent decision. Now people from all over the world could enjoy her treasures; and they would be well taken care of.

April introduced Mrs. Stewart to her grandson. The older woman looked at the baby and said, "He sure don't look like his father, but he is a fine boy."

Thank God for Daisy. She was the stabilizing force behind the family. Not only did she take guarded loving care of J.J., but she made sure that April and the Senator ate properly, their clothes were pressed and was better than a private secretary in steering them to their appointments. She anticipated their every need. Daisy was undoubtable the most wonderful person April had ever encountered in her whole life.

There was a meeting in a couple of hours at the woman's club that April was scheduled to speak. As she was putting on her makeup, she felt extremely nauseous. Must have a touch of the flu, she thought, or it could just be nerves.

The civil rights issue was being discussed everywhere. April felt very confident in saying that her husband was elected to serve ALL the good people of Georgia, not just a majority. He truly supported the constitution which guaranteed every person freedom of speech and religion. "There will be great strides for women in the future," she added. While she was speaking, she couldn't help but notice that the whole audience was white.

Several questions were asked and April grounded them carefully and as directly as possible. She had the impression that some of these women were totally against equal rights. They did not want their children going to school with black children. All of their husbands were prominent businessmen in the area. Bet they don't discriminate against selling and renting to blacks, she thought. How on earth could they continue to expect to keep a whole race from becoming educated and break the chains their very own ancestors had put on these people? It all seemed so foolish to her.

She met Jason back at the hotel, spent as much time as possible with J. J. and told Daisy that she felt she might have offended some of the women at the meeting today.

Daisy said, 'Betty, you gotta do what you gotta do." The Senator knew that he could not represent only the white voters when he took office. There's been a need for change for years. These old bones of mine say there is going to be a lot of people hurt before the Nation recognizes black people as citizens and equal to any man, regardless of color. All of the current generations of blacks have been born here on free soil. By law they are American citizens which means they are entitled to protection under the Constitution. There's already some marching going on in Alabama and the atmosphere is beginning to look violent. Shame, damn shame it has come to this."

April agreed. She was soaking in the tub when Jason came in dressed in his formal attire. There was a political dinner tonight at the country club to raise money for his campaign. Tired as she was, April got out of the tub and began the motions of getting dressed. Again, she was consumed by nausea. Carefully she brushed her hair and tried not to let Daisy or Jason see her face.

The event was one of many that seemed to be repeated hundreds of times throughout their stay in Georgia. Jason talked, they both shook hundreds of hands and ate cold meals. Just once, thought April, I wish I could have Daisy cook for us. Tomorrow they began their tour around the state. It had been agreed that Daisy would stay in Atlanta with some of her folks and keep little J.J. with her. If the trip had bothered him in any way, he surely didn't show it. He had already proven himself to be a hearty little traveler. April hated being parted from him, but knew that Daisy would put her own life on the line for that baby.

After an extremely long day of traveling, speaking, and meeting with campaign managers, Jason and April fell into bed exhausted. During the night, April became nauseous once again, and while she was in the bathroom, Jason got up and came in behind her.

"Darling, what's wrong," he asked.

"It must have been something I ate," she said.

They returned to bed and April spent the rest of the night in his arms. Even though she wanted more children, it was too soon. What if she lost this baby? She hadn't been to the doctor yet, but she knew the symptoms. She was inwardly thrilled to be carrying Jason's child, but she didn't want to tell him just yet. She wanted to be positive.

"Please God," she prayed, "please let this child be healthy and if its not too much trouble, please let it be a boy." She wanted more than anything in life to give Jason a biological son.

Everywhere they went it seemed that the only people who showed up at the rally's were white people. If there were any blacks, they just stood in the back and didn't ask any questions. April mentioned this to Jason in the limo on the way to another engagement. He didn't seem so concerned.

"They know my schedule," he said. "If they want representation, they should be interested enough to approach me with some of their problems. Certainly I would entertain their representatives, listen to their problems and try to approach a working solution. There was been an ill wind blowing throughout the South recently and many of my colleagues have stated they anticipated riots and blood shed prior to the next election."

"Jason, what I am hearing is unforgivable. You are saying that if you ignore this problem, it will just go away," said April.

"Darling, I am only saying that if it doesn't present itself as a problem, don't make one out of it."

April was shocked and angry. "Jason Stewart, you took an oath to support all the people of Georgia. How on earth can you sit here and tell me you choose to ignore an injustice that you have some control over?"

"Darling," said Jason. "You didn't grow up in the south, so you just don't understand the unique problems that arise here. Please don't get upset about it."

April was furious. "I may not have grown up in the south, but I know trouble brewing when I see it. Jason, I beg of you to campaign on the behalf of civil rights. Jump in now ahead of the riots and state your position. Let ALL the people know how you feel. Tell them you are not supporting the majority WASP. You have it in your power today to prevent problems you will have to face later if you are reelected. Set a precedence. Let the State of Georgia be an example the other states can look to for a smooth transition in the race issue.

"Darling, I have prepared speeches for every place on the tour. It's too late to alter them now. Just don't get so worked up about nothing."

April exploded! "Nothing! You call this issue nothing! Of all the things I ever felt about you, bigotry was not included. You of all people, have been conveniently lying to the very people you represent. You really don't give a damn about the black people of this state, do you? Seeing how Daisy has devoted her whole life to you, do you see her as a slave? She genuinely loves you and your family. She firmly believes she is a member of the family. Do you not see her black skin when you look at her, or do you just see good old Daisy, a black woman with no rights? Is she too dumb to vote, too ignorant to want the best representation for her people as well as the white people of this State? I think not, Jason Stewart."

"John would lay his life down for you. Is he just another slave, or is he just a black man who got lucky and found a job driving a big important U. S. Senator around town?"

Jason become a little angry with April. He said, "I can't believe you feel this strongly about an issue you truly know nothing about. If it makes you feel better, I'll have a talk with my campaign manager and see what he advises."

April refused to be appeased. Angrily she said, "Why don't you just do that Senator? Why don't you speak those gifted words that some well paid speech writer put down on paper for you. Let them manipulate you, if you want. However, they are not running for office Jason. I thought you were. Remember the people are not voting for your campaign manager. If you choose to continue to ignore this problem, your opponent will roll over you in this election if he defends the civil rights bill and votes for bussing."

"Please April, lets not go on and on about this, after we get home tonight, we can discuss it further."

Old John had heard the whole conversation. He couldn't wait to get back home and tell Daisy what he had heard. Never before in his employment with the Senator had he heard Betty be so adamant about anything. She sure was steamed today. It's about time she made her opinions known. He had always viewed her as a disinterested party. She had accomplished her goals in marrying an important man and then decided to sit back and enjoy it. Doing only what was absolutely necessary to contribute to his position.

April slid across the seat from Jason. Stupid Jackass, she thought. Maybe I misjudged him. Well, this is the first attempt to get involved in his politics. It's possible he always felt like this and I am the ignorant one. Not likely, she reasoned. No one in the world today could expect to keep a whole race of people in bondage.

The night seemed to drag. April tried to be cheerful, but it was difficult. She was out of sorts with Jason and her stomach was rolling uncomfortably.

Jason's speech was all he said it would be. Speeches and promises made to the white affluent crowd. After all, they were the only ones in the audience with the hundreds of dollars for the fund raising dinner. The only black faces April saw were the waiters and bartenders. It made her ill.

When they finally arrived back at the hotel. April called to check on little J.J., she talked to Daisy on the telephone. "Daisy, please tell me your honest opinion of my husband, Senator Stewart. Do you now or have you ever felt that he was prejudiced against blacks?"

It was obvious that Daisy was not prepared for this question. She hesitated and then replied. "Dahlin, you got to realize the Senator ain't never been part of the world you and I know exists. His daddy owns half of Georgia in real estate and his mama is the heir to the famed Rivers Furniture Estate. When his folks found out they was finally gonna have a baby, they done planned its life from birth to grave. Owning part interest in several newspapers, they primed the readers of Georgia about every major event in his life. How he was accepted to this school, how he was on the honor roll. Every accomplishment in his life was a milestone for them. That man ain't never seen share croppers, let alone see how they live. He jist don't understand that most young black kids in his state ain't never seen a tennis racket. Jason ain't never gone to bed hungry. He ain't never missed school cause his folks can't afford a doctor. He don't know that black kids that do go to school use such outdated material that it ain't possible for them to graduate with equal knowledge. I reckon darling he can't be blamed for something he jist don't know about. Anyways, why you calling me and asking 'bout all this?"

"Daisy, I think he should include something in his speeches in support of bussing and integration. Georgia is not a state that can ignore this issue. If Jason gets on the bandwagon now, he can surely pull more votes than his opponents. But, no matter how hard I try to push him in this direction, he won't budge. Are you sure you think its only ignorance and lack of exposure and not some young snob getting elected on his good looks and family name?"

Daisy was shocked. "Baby, you can be sure, he jist don't know. Take old Daisy's word for it. I know its true cause I raised this boy from birth. I seen how they protected him. He's my boy, but I can't be none too proud of him if he won't listen to you. What you're trying to do is right. Just hang in there darling, he'll come around."

April didn't feel much better when she hung up. She didn't want Jason to lose the election over this issue. As Jason entered the room, April hurriedly excused herself and ran into the bathroom. Again Jason followed. "'Betty, are you sure you're all right? Do you want me to get you a doctor, you seem to be sick a lot lately."

Turning around, April took a long look at this man standing in front of her. She loved him so much. Finally she said, "Jason, I can't keep it a secret forever. We are going to have a little playmate for J. J. I know it's soon, but when you flew out to Boulder and we made love that first night, I knew."

Jason's face lit up. "Darling, oh Betty, are you sure? Oh God, this is the greatest news I have had in a month. Do you want to go back home and let me campaign alone? Do you think the strain will cause any problems? Oh Betty, another baby. Thank you, thank you. I can hardly wait. I don't even care if it's a girl this time. We have a fine son already. Kissing her, he said. "I just can't believe my good fortune."

With this, he picked her up and delicately placed her on the bed. "From this day forward, you just say the word and your wish will be granted." Laying down beside her, he gave her a long and passionate kiss.

April started to say something about civil rights, but decided this was not the time or place.

11

SURPRISE VISITOR

Jason had some early appointments with his campaign managers, so April lounged in bed until after nine. She did not have any speeches today and didn't have to get dressed until tonight, if she desired. There was a fund raiser at some influential businessman's home. So far, the fund raising had gone quite well. Donations certainly didn't seem to be a problem.

April was surprised when she heard the knock on the door. Grabbing a robe, she answered. There stood Daisy and little J. J. A more beautiful sight she was sure she had never seen before. "Daisy, oh Daisy, how wonderful of you to come to Macon. You must be tired. Come on in and let me help you with all this junk. Do sit down and rest. I am so delighted to see you and my little darling boy."

Daisy said, "Miss Betty, I come because I thought about our last phone conversation. Also when the Senator sent John to come to pick us up, I decided to bring this nice gentleman along with me to talk to the Senator. Knowing how involved you are with his campaign, I persuaded Mr. William Miller to come with me. He's got a problem that I think you can help him with. I told him it don't matter whether he votes for the Senator or not."

An elderly black gentleman stepped into the room. Daisy introduced him to April. They shook hands and April excused herself so she could hurriedly dress and brush her hair. She instructed Mr. Miller to please make himself comfortable.

Daisy had, as usual, taken charge. She make sure Mr. Miller was seated. Then she called room service for refreshments.

Returning to the sitting room of the hotel, April saw that coffee and sweet rolls had been delivered.

"Now," she said, "Mr. Miller, I would like to hear about your problem."

"Miss I don't want to be no burden. But the more I thought about it, the madder I got. When Daisy heard about it, she said she knew just the person to fix it."

April readily agreed that Daisy was probably right, as usual.

The old man continued. "Me and my Bertha always made our own way in this world. We birthed and raised fourteen children on a sharecroppers wages and educated all of them best we could. Side by side, me and that woman and children worked from sun up to sun down and everyday, we thanked God for our bounty, sparse as it was. Bertha always had one wish and I promised her that it would come true. She went down to the funeral home in Atlanta and took out some burial insurance when we first got married. She paid the man seventy five cents a week for more than thirty five years. Sometime she walked to town, fifteen miles alone to give that man the precious money she always seemed to hold out of her pitiful wages. "It is only fittin and proper that black people be given a casket and decent funeral," she always said. My Bertha believed that this bit of luxury, or her piece of satin and silk, she called it, was the first step into another world devoid of wanting, such as this one."

"Well, a week ago, my Bertha died. I went down to the funeral home and showed the man the little book Bertha always kept of payments with his initials beside every entry. The man shouted at me that he ain't never received a penny from no black woman named Bertha Miller and that I better leave his establishment."

April saw how difficult it was for the elderly gentleman to continue. "Please have some more coffee Mr. Miller, and continue whenever you wish," she said.

"Well miss, I went home and got two of my older boys. We went down to the Sheriff's office. We told him what had happened and showed him the book. The Sheriff told us he couldn't do nothing to Mr. Higgins cause he hadn't broken no law."

"My boys got pretty upset and they told the Sheriff that he would hear from them again. He asked if they was threatening him. They said no, but their father had been cheated and they wouldn't rest until right was made right. With or without the help of the law."

"We went on home and built a box and took Bertha's body and wrapped it in one of her piecework quilts and put her to rest in the back of the old blacks graveyard. But miss, I can't sleep knowing that the woman done without finery for years and always scrimped to pay that insurance. Then when the poor woman died, she got cheated out of her lifelong dream of silk and satin."

"Mr. Miller, did you come up alone or did you bring one of your children with you?

"Miss, my sons was so fired up, they told me that no big Senator would give a damn about some poor black sharecroppers wife. "Why waste time," they said. "Just chalk up another whitey walk over. Miss, I don't mean to be disrespectful, but knowing how they feel, I thought it best if I didn't tell them I was gonna try one last shot to make it right for my Bertha."

"Mr. Miller," said April. "I promise you that you will be hearing from me soon. Unfortunately there are good and bad white people. Perhaps you could call one of your sons and have then come to see me and we can work together in getting this situation taken care of. You seem so tired, let me book you a room in the hotel and then you can telephone your family. When they arrive, I'll see that they have accommodations also."

The old gentleman lowered his head. "Miss, I don't want no trouble and I appreciate what your trying to do for me, but no fine hotel like this is going to rent me a room. I sure am tired, but I'll find me a place to sleep. My shack don't have no phone, so I'll get me some rest, then I'll catch a bus and head back home. I sure do thank you for your time though, I truly do."

As he rose to leave, April stood in front of him. "Mr. Miller, you came to me and asked for my help. Yet when I offered it, you refused. I said I would get you a room in this hotel and I will. Just stay put while I phone the desk."

April picked up the telephone and called down to the desk. "This is Senator Stewart's wife, I need a single immediately for a guest that has just arrived. The gentlemen's name is William Miller and is in my suite presently. If you would send someone up with a key, I would appreciate it greatly."

Again April picked up the telephone, she called Jason's campaign headquarters. When she finally got through to him, she said she needed one of his people that could be trusted to drive to Atlanta and bring someone back with them. Because Jason was busy and had people pulling him in thirty direction, he said he would send someone right over and hung up.

A knock on the door brought a bell boy with a room key. When he saw Mr. Miller was black, he did not hesitate to state that it was hotel policy that no blacks could room there.

April was livid. "If you refuse a room to Mr. Miller, tell your manager to send up some bell captains to have the Senator and myself moved to a hotel that does not have color as a requirement for lodging."

It only took a few minutes before the manager appeared in the suite and said he thought there had been a misunderstanding. Of course they would comply with Mrs. Stewart's wishes and find her guest a room.

Turning to the bell boy, the manager handed the bell boy a key and said, "I am sure that this key to room 1207 will be suitable to Mr. Miller."

Daisy had been sitting holding little J.J taking all this in. She chuckled softly. "That man done got his buns in trouble," she said. "Miss Betty, you sure gave him a snoot full of his own snobbery. Lawd I wish the Senator could have seen how heat up you was. I never knowed you had such a temper."

Taking her baby in her arms, April saw Daisy and Mr. Miller to the elevator. Daisy was not going to let Mr. Miller roam around the hotel alone. She had brought the problem to Miss Betty and was going to see it through with her. Only when she was sure that the ole man was comfortable did she leave. She showed him how to use the telephone to call her or the senator's suite if he needed anything. Also, she said she would come back later and check on him. For now, he needed to get some rest.

Daisy arrived just as the young worker from Jason's campaign office did. She heard Betty telling the young man that she wanted him to drive to a residence outside of Atlanta and pick up a friend of hers and deliver him back to this suite. She asked if the volunteer had any racial feelings about going into the home of a black person. After being assured that there was no bias, she gave the directions and asked them to return to Macon as soon as humanly possible.

The young man left with his instructions and Daisy vowed to be there when he returned. The young man was a college student and reminded her of Jason. Jumping on every bandwagon to get his name attached to influential people, hoping it would somehow enhance their own dreams of the future.

April was on the telephone again. This time she called the courthouse in Atlanta. After identifying herself to the clerk, she asked for someone to check the tax records of the Higgins Funeral Home. Were they possibly in arrears? The person on the other end agreed to search the file personally and to return the call as soon as possible. They were so excited that a Senator's wife had called them.

It wasn't long before she got her answer. There were back taxes owed in the amount of $63,846.07. The reason for the delinquent taxes was the Higgins Funeral Home was the only funeral Home within sixty miles of any other facility. Therefore it was continuously overlooked because of the service it provided. Also, Higgins liked betting on the races. When April hung up, after thanking the public servant for their help, she had a smile on her face that was devious and challenging. Daisy didn't say anything. She liked what she saw. Until now, Betty had never exhibited such a fighting spirit before in her marriage to Jason. Come to think of it, she never got involved in anything Jason ever did but parties, she thought. Well, I like what I see.

April called the District Attorney's Office and after identifying herself, asked why the taxes were so delinquent on the Higgins Funeral Home. She didn't ask that Mr. Higgins be prosecuted but her hint was so blunt that if no action was taken, it would strongly be noted by the Senator of the State.

Next April asked Daisy if she knew a good lawyer that would handle affairs discreetly. One that would not show prejudice if it involved dealing with blacks.

Daisy said that one of Jason's friends was very competent. He was in Jason's circle of friends not because of family wealth because there wasn't any, but because he was such a good and honest person. He had worked his way through college and taken all honors available to boot. This is how April met Jack Adams. He agreed to meet her over lunch. April hung up the telephone and rushed to get dressed presentable enough for the luncheon. Her hair was a mess and her appointment to have it styled was around four. Well, she thought, as she brushed it, 'I'll just put a scarf on and go casual."

Jack Adams was a very pleasant person. He refused a cocktail which endured him immediately to April. Most people would have taken this luncheon as an excuse to wine and dine in extravagance.

"Tell me what your problem is Mrs. Stewart as I have a calendar full of events this afternoon. You said the magic word when you mentioned lunch. It's the only free time I have open for six months."

April liked the straight forwardness. "Mr. Adams, I have a problem that I wish straightened out. A friend of mine has been swindled by a prominent citizen in Atlanta and I wish to see justice right this terrible wrong."

Between bites, April related the story to Jack Adams as Mr. Williams had told it to her.

"Now Mrs. Stewart, I can see that you want more than justice served. What do you really want to happen from this incident?"

"Mr. Adams, you have seen through my devious plan. Indeed I do want more than Mr. Higgins brought up on charges of tax violation. I want to pay those taxes and become a silent partner in his operation, controlling interest, of course."

"Jack Adams let out a laugh that caused several patrons to stare. "That's good, really good. Lady I like your style. However I fail to see how this will strike a blow to the Higgins Funeral Home."

"I am coming to that," said April. "You see, I want my partnership to be in the name of two of Mr. Williams's sons. I want to buy a full partnership which includes the tax amount. However…" Before she could finish the sentence, Jack Adams laughed again and said, "You don't want Higgins to know that you have set him up with two black partners until he agrees to someone paying his taxes and offering him a fair price for a full partnership. Am I correct?"

"Mr. Adams, I see I was correct in asking for your assistance. Now, the Williams' are proud people and I do not want to embarrass them with this opportunity as I feel very strongly that they would refuse a gift. So, if you could somehow set up a pay back method that is suitable to them for however many years it takes to pay back, I would appreciate it. Shall we say at two percent interest?

Jack Adams assured April that he would be in touch. "You know, if the Senator showed as much interest in man kind as you obviously do, he wouldn't have to campaign so hard. He sure got himself a winner when he got you." Shaking April's hand he said, "It will be a pleasure to serve you mam."

April arrived back at the hotel. She spent a few minutes with little J.J. Daisy told her that the young campaign worker had arrived back with two of Mr. William's sons. April thanked her and asked the room number again. Then she took the elevator to meet Mr. Williams's sons.

The two sons were images of their father. There was a outdoors look about them, but intelligence in their faces.

"Gentlemen, I have some good news and some bad news," she said. First I have alerted the District Attorney's office about the Higgins Funeral Home being in arrears for back taxes. Then I consulted a lawyer and asked to allow me to pay the delinquent taxes. A full partnership will be established in your names to assure that no person, black or white will be swindled again. I saw no gain in having Mr. Higgins jailed. So, I want you two to take over management of the place and let Mr. Higgins be your front man or figure head. He does have the reputation, such as it is, and you will have to accept the fact that at this very moment, being black does not have the advantage of allowing you to run the place on your own. Mr. Higgins will have to eat humble pie for the rest of his entire life if we play our cards right."

The whole time April was speaking, she was watching the reactions on their faces. "You think there's a catch to this, don't you. I can see the suspicion on your faces. Well, this is no gift. You will have to work hard and I expect the loan I am going to make you be paid in full at agreeable terms. My lawyer, a Mr. Jack Adams is currently working out the details. If you will contact him, I feel sure this can all be worked out to everyone's satisfaction.

There were tears in old Mr. Williams' eyes. "Daisy done said you was a good woman, but I thought she was jist saying this cause she worked for you. I can see now why she thinks so highly of you," he said.

April stayed and answered as many questions as possible and assured that the sons did indeed want the chance. Rufus and Bo stated that they could indeed handle the management of the place with no problems. First they would find out who had been cheated and make it right with all the folks they could find. Then they would work toward giving people their money's worth without taking undue advantage of their grief.

April had to run to keep her hair appointment. She wanted to look special for Jason tonight. She hadn't realized just how involved this day had been. And, she through, this was one of my light days. Daisy's being there and bringing little J.J. had brightened her outlook on life.

Jason was in the room getting dressed when April returned from the hairdressers. After getting a big hug and kiss, Jason asked her about her day. She had a huge grin on her face and said, "Just routine darling, just routine." Daisy just shook her head and hid her smile. "Bless that chile, Lord," she said softly. 'Bless that chile."

That evening the party was loud and like so many others they had attended. April loved campaigning but thought some originality should go into these bashes instead of just drinking too much and eating bad food.

Jason was introducing her around when April spotted a familiar face. Jason started to introduce her to Jack Adams. Before he could begin, Jack smiled and said, "We've met. Senator you have a most gracious, charming and warm hearted person for a wife. I truly envy you sir."

Jason was going to comment, but there was no time. He was interrupted and left April alone with Jack Adams.

"You sure stirred up a nest of hornets lady. I called the District of Attorney told him that I had an interested party who would not only like to pay back the back taxes for Higgins, but who wanted to become a full partner. Higgins is in deep financial trouble and didn't even ask who. He just agreed to any terms that the D.A. and I think are adequate to sustain his business and avoid prosecution. I sure would like to see the look on Hadley Higgins face when he discovers that he has sold out to blacks. He will have a fit."

Again April thanked Jack Adams and gave him a blank check with her signature on it. "Fill in whatever amount it takes to make this situation workable and profitable to the two Williams'." Reaching into her little beaded bag, she took out a white envelope and handed it to Jack Adams. "This sir, is for your support, assistance and discretion. I do hope you will allow me to call on you again if I encounter any other problems while I am in this area."

"Agreed," he said, taking the envelope. Shaking hands, they parted.

12

THE ARREST

April was tired to the bone. Also she was having nausea more than ever. Maybe its my nerves, she thought. Daisy was a all a flutter. She had warned Betty that if she didn't slow down, there could be trouble for her and the new baby. April put her off saying that she had to campaign for her husband and that is what she was going to do. Maybe she could rearrange her schedule though to give herself more rest.

Picking up the paper and finding that Serena and Max Hartley were making their bid for the Senate this year and that it looked favorable did not help her attitude. With his luck and her good looks, they'll surely win, she thought. Well, if that's the will of the people, so be it.

When she arrived at the ladies luncheon, April saw her first signs of protest. There were twenty or thirty black people protesting the establishment for not allowing them equal access to the facilities. When John let her out of the limo, there were angry words shouted to her. April was shocked. Well, she had warned Jason, if he didn't get involved soon, he would lose for sure.

April went over to the crowd. John tried to stop her as well as the aid that Jason insisted accompany her everywhere she went.

April shouted for the protesters to be quiet. "If this establishment will not admit all Americans, regardless of the color of their skin, then I shall not enter it either."

There was a loud cheering and April stepped into the picket line formed by the protesters. She continues, "If we are all American's then let us be treated equally and justly. This grand country can no longer ignore the wealth of the oppressed. The constitution guarantees all men equal rights regardless of his color. Stand up for your rights for fair representation by your elected officials. Use the power of your vote to gain for yourselves the rights you so avidly want. Take whatever means you must to obtain what is legally yours by nature of your ancestry."

The crowd had grown. More and more people were joining the group that was picketing the segregated restaurant. Soon April discovered that there were TV cameras and newspaper men asking for and getting interviews from the people in the crowd. There were also some very angry people who had not joined the group voicing an opposite opinion. Some of it was directed at April. She was called "nigger lover, campaigning white princess who wants her husband to be reelected" and other names she chose to ignore. She walked the line with the protesters until the police arrived. They pulled up in their vehicles and just started clubbing people like they were dogs.

April was totally appalled by this action. John was struck on the head very violently trying to defend April. She turned to the policeman who had issued the blow and asked if they had thought about giving the people a chance to go to the jail peacefully, without all the unnecessary violence.

The policeman drew up his club to strike her when someone grabbed his arm. She saw that it was one of the Miller sons. He held the policeman's arm and "suggested" that the Senator's wife be escorted without harm.

Hearing that this woman was the Senator's wife, the policeman apologized over and over.

"I wish to be transported with the other protesters," April replied. Even though the police offered to release April, she refused.

April was taken to the police station. The TV camera's were rolling along with them. God, thought April, what have I gotten myself in for this time. Jason was not going to like this one bit. Well, she had made her decision and now she had no choice but to see it through. In her anger, she thought, to hell with Jason.

She was booked, photographed, fingerprinted and then put into a cell. This had to be the worse thing April had ever experienced in her life. She had had offers to be set free from everyone in the station. Still she held fast. "Free all the protesters, or lock me up with them," was her reply.

While the protesters were awaiting arraignment, the ones closest to April found out that she was not concerned about their vote as much as she was genuinely concerned about their rights. While they were in this small confined space, she reinforced her sincere feelings about segregation.

Jason arrived at the station to post bail for April. She asked him to accompany her to the court. He refused. It was clear that he was not going to involve himself in this situation. April would not yield. "Why don't you get back to whatever it is that you find so important," she said. "It's obviously not the plight of the oppressed in your state."

April had tears in her eyes as Jason walked out of the jail. Well, she couldn't change the current events now, she had to go through with them.

The judge sat on his bench in his black ceremonial robes and proceeded to lecture the group of protesters.

April was angry, needed a bath, and her stomach was churning. "Your honor, please spare us your bias opinions and set bail. I for one would like to get out of this court of injustice."

The judge turned purple. The protesters cheered. Pounding on the desk, the judge restored order. "Young lady, I don't care if you are the wife of a prominent Senator from this grand state, I find you in contempt."

"Fine," said April. "Just spare me your prejudiced opinion. I'll gladly pay whatever fine you see fit. However, I would like for you to keep it within reason. The hallway is full of TV and Newspaper Reporters anxious to hear how you treated all the protesters. Oh yes, and remember that it's an election year. I wonder how many votes you have in this group standing here today?"

The crowd clapped and cheered.

"Bailiff," barked the judge. "Please clear the courtroom. This court is adjourned."

The crowd gathered around April and thanked her for her assistance. She tried so hard to share their enthusiasm but she felt so very very ill. Searching the crowd she saw John as he tried to weed his way over to her. He arrived at her side and took her arm. "Jist you lean on Ole John," he said. "I'll see to it that you gets back to the hotel, don't you worry bout nothing."

Somehow John managed to get April back to the hotel. There were reporters everywhere. She pushed through them and got up to the suite. Jason was not there. Thank God for that she thought as she fell asleep. She was so exhausted.

Daisy had taken charge again. She told the desk to put no calls through, she didn't care of it was the President hisself.

Next she insisted that John go to the hospital and get some stitches in his wound. It sure did look bad. He had not received any medical attention whatsoever in jail. This done, she went into the bedroom and undressed April. The poor child sure was stubborn, she thought, but I am so proud of her.

Jason came into the suite. Daisy, hearing the door shut, came hurrying in to greet him. "Damn you Senator," she said. "How could you walk away from this poor little thing who wants nothing more than to help your career? You gonna lose that wonderful little girl in there if you don't take your head out of the sand and get with the real world."

Jason was shocked. Daisy had never raised her voice to him. She was hot as a pistol right now though.

"Daisy, help me, I..."

They both heard the small call for help at the same time. Daisy ran back into the bedroom and saw that April was trying to sit up. She was hysterical and saying, "The baby, Oh God Jason I am so sorry, the baby."

Daisy saw the blood. This poor child was hemorrhaging badly. She almost knocked Jason over getting to the telephone. After directing the desk to send an ambulance up to their suite for an emergency, Daisy returned to April's side. Taking her in her arms, she said, "Betty, oh chile, jist you hang on. Daisy will take care of you. That baby is gonna just be fine. You jist trust old Daisy."

Jason stood by and watched. His heart ached. What on earth could he do. He hoped that this baby would survive. He loved this woman so much it hurt to see her in such pain. What could he do to make this up to her? She looked so fragile in Daisy's arms. Where did she get all these ideas from all of a sudden, he wondered. Why was she so adamant about this civil rights issue? She hadn't grown up in this State, why was she getting so involved in a problem that was clearly not hers?

As the ambulance arrived and April was transported to the hospital, the TV cameras were recording every minute of it. Jason was asked to comment. "Was this brought on because of her going to jail? "Was she mistreated while in jail?" There were hundreds of questions. Jason just muttered, "No comment."

On the drive to the hospital, his heart was breaking for her. He loved her so very very much. She had given him meaning since her return from Boulder after the plane crash. He had told no one that she went home to reconsider their marriage. Since her return, it seemed that she had made her choice and it had been a good choice. She had survived the crash, the surgery's, had a beautiful son and was now beside him and behind him in his campaign. They had had the best part of their married life together after the accident. She seemed so much more vital, and they were so in love again. Their sex life had improved two hundred percent and she had stated that she wanted to give him a house filled with little love children. An extension of their lives together. A creation of love. Before the crash, she had not wanted children. Her father must have really straightened her out, he thought. Now, she was again fighting for her life and the life of this baby she wanted so badly. He prayed that she would survive this ordeal and come back to him whole as before.

The doctors told Jason that it would be twenty four hours before they would know about the baby. So far she had not aborted. When she was conscious, she made it clear that this child was going to make it. She kept repeating over and over, "This is Jason's child, his son, I must not fail him. God forgive me for my sins, but spare the child."

Jason stated that he knew she wanted children badly. Their son J.J. had enhanced their lives so much. It was probably that Betty was such a fighter that she refused to be defeated by nature, he thought. She was certainly a different person since she came back from Boulder.

Daisy arrived at the hospital. She had made arrangements for her cousin to come to the hotel and take care of J.J. She felt she was needed here at the hospital. April was unaware that the hand she held all night belonged not to her beloved husband, but her loyal friend and servant. Daisy prayed all night for God to spare this sweet child and her unborn infant.

Jason had reluctantly attended all the functions previously scheduled for that evening. His appearance was one of a man without spark. For the first time in a long time, he felt the emptiness beside him where the beloved Betty should have been. He felt the oppression of realizing just how dear she was to him. How they had put so much living into so little time. He would make it up to her, he vowed. He would somehow make it up to her, somehow he made it through the evening.

Arriving back at the hotel he found his son with a stranger. When he was told that Daisy had taken his place at the hospital, he felt like crying. Daisy had taken his place just as Betty had taken it in the civil rights uprising.

He picked up the telephone and called John's room. Shortly John came in and Jason asked him to sit down. He wanted to talk. He wanted John to be open and honest in his opinions. He needed to hear the truth.

John was candid in the beginning, however he told Jason about the inadequacies of eating, sleeping and shopping facilities available to black patrons. About busses, bathrooms, schools and churches that banned blacks to spaces especially set aside for them. John spoke of how he was allowed to stay in a small room in the basement of this hotel only because he was the Senator's chauffeur. He could not enter the bar or restaurant areas. When he wanted to eat, he had to travel across town to the black areas to get food.

Jason listened with sincere interest. As he had never encountered any of these incidents, he was appalled. John was telling him exactly what Betty and Daisy had been trying to tell him all along.

Jason asked John if he minded driving him to the hospital. He made sure that his loving son was safe before he left. He felt an uncontrollable desire to be with his wonderful wife at this time.

There were crowds of people on the sidewalks, the corridors and the waiting rooms. They were black and white sitting silently praying. An orderly came over to the Senator and told him that after the six o'clock news report that the Senator's wife was in the hospital, small groups began to form asking if they could keep a vigil. They had been there since and insisted on staying until they knew she was out of danger.

Jason thanked all of them for coming and being there when he and his wife needed support. This was a speech he said freely and from his heart. Later he thought about what his campaign manager would say. To hell with my campaign manager, he thought. Betty was right, I need to get down with the people more, talk to them instead of making some long winded speech that was written by someone else. He vowed to change the remainder of his campaign.

It was around four A.M. when the doctor found Jason half asleep on a bench in the waiting room. He told him loud enough for everyone to hear that Mrs. Stewart seemed to be out of trouble and wanted to see her husband as soon as possible.

Jason almost broke his leg getting into the room. Daisy got up to leave. "Stay Daisy, I think you might want to hear what I have to say. Betty says you are a part of our family and what I have to say is for the family."

April smiled. "Darling, the doctor says you are going to be okay. The baby seems to be hanging on too. John and I had a long talk tonight about the issues you have been trying to tell me about. Betty you were right. These things I am hearing are not to be allowed to continue in existence. Tomorrow, or later today, I should say, you will find a more intense, better educated Senator going through the State speaking on people's rights. These speeches won't be made just to the people who have these rights anymore. I'll throw away my speeches and speak from the heart. We'll see if you can be proud of me again."

"Jason, darling. I have always been proud of you. My God man, I love you."

April drifted off again. Jason asked Daisy to return to the hotel. He said that Betty seemed to be in good hands and with hundreds of people praying for her, she had to get better. It would ease his mind if he knew that his son was with someone he was used to. Right at this time in their lives, the baby didn't need to be upset by having strangers enter his life. He needed a competent sitter and someone who loved him.

Jason continued his campaign while April remained in Macon convalescing. She had had several transfusions and there were hundreds of volunteers to give blood if she needed more. The doctor told her how lucky she was that she had not miscarried. Her heart was broken when she discovered that she could not finish the campaign with Jason. Well, her efforts had not been futile.

13

THE ELECTION NIGHT

April had been allowed to return to the hotel. She refused to leave Jason in Georgia and fly home to Maryland. Jason said he would watch the results from the suite verses the campaign headquarters. He wanted to remain close to Betty.

The early results were good. "I hope he didn't wait too long to start his campaigning from the heart," thought April. He was a good man and he took great pride in his position. She knew that his second term would be much harder now though that the civil rights issue were becoming full blown. He could handle it, she thought.

Sandwiches and drinks were continuously being served to the people who were crowded into the adjoining room of the suite. This room had previously served as Daisy's and little J.J.'s room. April and the baby were in the bedroom with the door closed. J.J. needed his rest and so did April. There were continuous reports from people who were relaying messages from headquarters to the suite. Jason was ahead by a small margin.

The results from the race in Missouri showed Congressman Hartley ahead in his race for the Senate. Jason relayed this information to Betty. She tried not to show any emotion what so ever. Surprisingly, she wasn't bitter. However, she hated having Max and Serena so close to her and her family. Even though Max didn't know it, he would always be a real threat to April's happiness.

It seemed to take forever before the final results were tallied. It had been a close race but Jason had won by a small margin. He managed to swing some of the black vote in his direction. Unfortunately not all blacks could vote due to some stupid rules and tests they were required to take. He vowed to look into this and see what pressure he could exert on the governor to make some changes in this area.

Jason kissed April and said that he would try not to stay too long at the victory celebration. However he felt obligated to go. April insisted that she, J.J. and Daisy would be just fine. He needed to relax. She told him to have a good time. Then she gave him an extremely passionate kiss and congratulated him on his victory.

Daisy came into the bedroom with a bottle of champaign. "This one was left over. If you are up to it darling, we'll have our own little party."

April hated all alcoholic beverages, but didn't want to disappoint Daisy. She took a glass and they clinked them together and made a toast to the next term.

April was glad when they left Georgia. Now they could finally take possession of their new home. Jason could get back to his routine at work, Daisy would stop being so protective, and J.J. could roam around in his own spaces. No more hotel rooms and hotel food.

Two weeks after they moved into their new house, April insisted that the first people they would entertain would be the workers from Jason's office. The pool was covered over and April had some tents on the lawn to cover areas where people could sit. They had a wonderful turn out as everyone invited came. Their home was beautiful. April couldn't wait for Carolyn to return from campaigning so she could tell her how very pleased she was with her work. Also, she needed to pay her for this labor of love.

Assisting Daisy from the kitchen, April couldn't help but overhear part of a conversation. "She was really put out on the street, are you serious?"

When April saw that the two people gossiping were young secretaries from the typing pool, she couldn't help but ask who had been put on the street.

Gwen said that this young black girl Jason had hired recently was having financial difficulties. She had an illegitimate daughter and the Senator felt sorry for her and gave her a job. She was originally from Savannah. The baby had been sick and Claudette didn't have any hospitalization.

After she paid the hospital, she found that she couldn't pay the rent. She went home one day and found everything she owned was on the street. At least, whatever pitiful bit people hadn't helped themselves to. The landlord had already rented her apartment to someone else. The girl had applied for emergency welfare but in order to get it she would have to place the baby in a foster home. This just about destroyed Claudette. She had taken extra jobs at night in fast food places so she could save the money to get another apartment to bring the baby home to.

April asked Gwen to have Claudette get in touch with her.

"Maybe I can assist," she said.

Gwen agreed to have Claudette call. April could not shake this horror story from her mind all evening.

Their very first party in their new home had been a huge success. Daisy had outdone herself. She had insisted on making all the food herself instead of using a catering service. The extra help adored Daisy and almost anticipated her next move. They loved doing the big parties, they said.

J.J. was the life of the party. He had been picked up and held by so many people. Yet he continued to be charming and smiled as if on cue. April thought he was a little devil. "Campaigning already aren't you," she asked? Can't have you upstaging your daddy though, so she put him to bed.

Jason told April that he was extremely proud of his wife tonight. "Everything was absolutely perfect. The house, the meal, the baby. By the way, he added, how did you train that little devil to be so charming," he asked?

April smiled at Jason and said, "It seems to be a family trait, my dear."

April told Daisy to go to bed. She would have some help come in tomorrow to help clean up. Daisy was beginning to slow down some. Well, who wouldn't, thought April. She raised Jason, takes care of me and the baby, keeps our lives running smoothly and supervises the rest of the staff. She ought to be tired.

Making a mental note, April decided that the time to promote Daisy to just companion and hire someone else to do all the other chores. She knew she would meet resistance when she discussed this with Daisy. Anyway, if she wasn't so busy all the time, she and Daisy could have more of their little chats sitting around in the kitchen. April had managed to extract information she was supposed to already know from Daisy very carefully in the past. She had been April's lifeboat throughout the deception.

14

CLAUDETTE

April called Claudette and was told that she should catch the bus or trolley and come right over. If she didn't have the fare, a car would be sent for her. She said that she could get there with no problem. April was surprised to see how thin this young woman was.

Daisy had made some small sandwiches and put out some cold drinks and a pot of coffee. She, April and Claudette sat around the kitchen table and talked. April thought this cozy setting would be less intimidating than using the formal living room.

April introduced herself and Daisy. "I heard from some of your co-workers that you are having a difficult time here in the Capitol City," said April.

Big tears fell down the young girls cheeks. "Me and my baby come here cause we thought I could find some work. I wanted something more than a living in a shack and picking cotton and peaches. I saved up all season and bought a ticket. When I got here I went to the Senator's office and asked if they needed a hard worker who was willing to do anything. This even included cleaning the toilets if necessary."

"The Senator was standing there and heard my speech. He told the lady out front to find a spot for me. I was so grateful. In my purse was just enough money to buy the baby some milk for supper. I went to the YMCA on "K" Street like I was told. They verified that I had a job and allowed me to stay with a promise I would pay them out of my first check."

"They didn't allow babies, but seeing how I was so desperate, there was a kind lady there that said she would watch Penelope for me. She loved kids and was bored. She even offered to feed me and Penny until I could get settled."

"I tole her I would try and pay her back as soon as I got a check. So everyday

I got up and bathed myself and baby and walked to the Senate Office to work."

"Everything seemed to be going fine until Penelope got sick: She caught pneumonia and had to be hospitalized. I think it was the air conditioning, cause we ain't never had air conditioning before. Anyway, I had saved enough money for a deposit on a furnished apartment and paid the first month's rent. I had found a used baby bed, and moved our clothes in. There was pots and pans and dishes already there."

"When I went to the hospital to bring Penny home, the woman in the credit department said they wouldn't give me my baby if I didn't pay the bill right then and there. So I used the rent money. When me and Penny got to the apartment, everything we owned was out on the street. People was jist helping themselves to whatever they wanted. We didn't have much, but what we had was ours and it was clean."

"I didn't know what to do, so I took the baby and walked down to the bus station and set all night. First thing in the morning I found the welfare office and went down there. They tole me they would help me but only if I let them put Penelope in a foster home. This broke my heart but I didn't have no choice. I slept in the bus station for a week and took showers at the office. I waited each evening till everybody else left and I went into the Senator's bathroom and washed my clothes and myself. I sure hope he don't mind. I cleaned up every day afterwards."

April assured Claudette that Jason certainly wouldn't mind.

The tears were coming again. "'Claudette, do you have a place to stay now or are you still sleeping wherever you can," asked April.

"I put another deposit down on this place close to where I had the first apartment and I slept there yesterday. The welfare office won't let me have my baby back until they inspect the apartment. I know this apartment won't pass, but it's all I could afford. I jist know they is gonna take my baby away from me. I can't live without my baby."

"How would you like to come and stay with us for a while until you get settled," asked April? "We have plenty of room and J.J. would have company. In the meanwhile, I'll see what I can do to help you get settled proper, and help you get your baby back."

"You mean come and live her in this beautiful house," asked Claudette?

"That's exactly what she means chile," said Daisy. "We won't take no for an answer, will we Miss Betty?"

John was called to drive Claudette to her apartment to fetch her belongings. April got on the telephone to the welfare office and began the proceedings to have Penelope delivered to their house in Bethesda. She simply stated that Claudette had a permanent residence now and wished to have the baby delivered at the earliest possible convenience.

April excused herself and went to the bedroom and got dressed. She had called her lawyer on "K" street and had an appointment for 3 O'clock. If she hurried, she would be able to make it.

When April arrived, Mr. Carter ushered her into his office.

"What do I hear about your interest in buying property on East Capitol Street," he asked?

"What I want to do is to beautify and restore some of those old homes. I want you to find out who owns them and see if they are willing to sell. I plan to meet with some of the local officials and present my plan for restoration. There is money available for this and I intend to restore them and give some tenants an opportunity to own them at a low interest rate. I believe that if they have pride in their property it will be contagious and the whole block will improve. If however, the landlords don't sell, I intend to put pressure on them through the Mayor and the City Counsel to insist that they meet standards required by the city ordinances. No one should be forced to live in run down rat and roach infested traps and be charged outrageous rents. The hot water should work, and adequate heat should be available. I want to personally buy as many of these buildings as I can for this restoration purpose. Do you think you can help me?"

"Mrs. Stewart, are you sure you want to do this," asked Mr. Carter. "It will tie up your money for long periods of time without a return. Also, the interest will be so low when you find a qualified buyer that you may never recoup a profit. Have you thought about putting your money in, say, mutual funds?"

"Mr. Carter, I came here for your assistance, not your advice. Either you wish to engage me as a client or you don't. If not, I am sorry I wasted your time."

Henry Carter began quickly to apologize. "I am truly sorry if I offended you mam, but I feel it is in the best interest of my client's to advise them of the best situations as I see them. Of course I will assist you in this endeavor. Give me approximately one week and I will have something for you then. In the meanwhile if you have any questions, please feel free to call me or stop in."

He shook April's hand and said, "I'll be in touch."

April was so relieved when she got out of there. She realized that Jason's wealth exceeded even her comprehension. With the money left to her from Betty's inheritance, the least she could do was to use it to give something back.

April wandered over to Connecticut Avenue and did some shopping for J.J. a pretty scarf caught her eye and she bought that for Daisy. After carefully searching several men's stores, she found a few dress shirts for Jason. He never seemed to have time to buy clothes for himself. Several of the cuffs and collars were becoming frayed on some of his shirts. Daisy just usually called Raleigh's and told them to send over a dozen shirts in assorted colors and styles. What

Jason liked, he kept, the others were returned. April wondered about his real taste in clothes. He probably got so used to a domineering mother and loving Daisy making all these choices that he just never developed a like or dislike. He always seemed so eager to please everyone else.

When April arrived home, Claudette had moved into one of the spare bedrooms that had its own bath. She was walking on cloud nine. She had tears in her eyes when April showed her the sweaters she had bought for her.

Shortly after, there was a very severe lady who rang the bell and had a small black baby with her. This must be Penelope, thought April. She invited the lady in. One thing for sure, she was a complete snob. Bet she's pissed because this poor black woman has better living quarters that she has, though April. Oh well, life is a bitch.

Claudette was beside herself trying to please April. Daisy kept telling her to relax. The baby was well behaved and she and J.J. were having a ball crawling around on the carpet trying to get into everything in sight. J.J. exhibited a great curiosity about Penelope. He crawled over and touched her and said "baby." April was delighted. Now he wouldn't be jealous when the new baby arrived. Despite all the attention the little devil had been given, he seemed to remain unspoiled and lovable to all he encountered. He had that winning smile down pat.

After they had dinner, Claudette, April and Daisy sat down again around the kitchen table. Jason was in a late session at work and wouldn't be home until much later. The babies were asleep.

"Claudette, how would you like to go into business for yourself," asked April?

"Mam, that would be a dream come true. But what can I do? I don't even have a high school diploma and all I ever done is pick cotton and peaches. I can type some and I'm learning new things down at the Senator's office. What could I do on my own," she asked?

"What if I insisted that you enroll in adult courses here in town and get a GED that would be equivalent to a diploma? Then you can take a bookkeeping course and maybe some child care courses at one of the universities in the city? That way, you could get a loan, purchase a building that would allow for a nursery as well as live in quarters for you and Penelope. You could take care of other peoples babies while they work. This would allow you to be with Penelope all the time instead of part time. There's a real need for good child care in this city. Daisy and I are always trying to find adequate sitters for J.J. If you feel you want to do this, I will assist you 100%."

Claudette couldn't believe her ears. This kind lady was giving her an opportunity of a lifetime. How could she refuse?

"I'll work real hard Mrs. Stewart and make you proud of me," she said. It was hard to speak as her heart was pounding so hard. If it was a dream, she hoped never to wake up.

Claudette said good night and went to her bedroom. Daisy said, "Miss Betty, I don't know why you is helping this chile, but I am proud of you. She jist didn't have no place to turn to. Losing her baby was the final straw. She didn't have the money to stay and no money to go home on. You sure give her a dream. That chile is your friend all the rest of your life."

"Daisy," said April, "While we are talking and we are alone, I wanted to tell you something. My father left me a substantial amount of money as you know. Jason has asked me to use it as I see fit. God knows his family left enough for him and one hundred heirs to live a full extravagant life on. Since J.J. is crawling and soon to walk, and the new baby coming, I want you to slow down a bit. Just be a nanny instead of trying to run a household and keep our schedules. Now Daisy I don't mean to upset you, I just don't want anything to happen to you. Interfere where and when you see fit, but just don't try to do it all. You raised Jason, continuously pamper me, and are helping to raise our son."

Placing a bank book in Daisy's hand, April said, "I want to give you something back for all the years of loyal service. I went to the bank and established a fund for you. Use it as you see fit. Buy a home, take a vacation, do whatever you want, but please use it. Of course I want you with us for as long as we exist as a family. Please don't mistake what I am saying or doing. We love you Daisy, but you need a life too. Here's your chance at it. I can't begin to tell you how valuable your friendship to me has been. Your loving care and concern while I was sick and recuperating was invaluable. Money can't buy that kind of love or loyalty. Now I want to give you a gift. Please take it and use it however you wish.

Daisy took the book. There in big black figures was the amount of $100,000.00. "Lawd Miss Betty," she exclaimed. "I can't take this much money. What on earth would I do with it? Surely the bank made a mistake. I never in my lifetime expected to see that much money in one pile, let alone with my name on it."

"Daisy,"' said April. "I assure you that it's not a mistake. Perhaps you have some family you would like to visit or offer assistance to. Anyway, its yours old friend."

"Miss Betty, I don't know what happened to you after the plane crash, but I like you more now than ever before. It's not the money. When you went home to Boulder the first time, me and the Senator didn't know if you was coming back or not. Jason was scared. He thought the marriage was over too. You two had been so unhappy for such a long time. There was that big fight about starting a family. Jason always wanted babies, you didn't. If you could have seen his face when you called and said you was pregnant and was coming back, he turned pale and stood there with tears running down his face. He turned to me and said,

Daisy, its all right. She's coming home and we are going to have a baby."

"Having seen this man grow up and not really consider anyone's feelings but his own, this sight really shook me. He was getting a second chance and he was so happy. I been wanting to tell you how glad I am that you come back and that you come back full of love. There's been too much fighting in this house. He has finally realized that he can't take nothing for granted. He has to give as well as take. I wants to say thank you for making his life so full and so happy. Since I ain't never had no children, I feel like he's my chile as I raised him. Now I gets to help with his babies. You jist don't know how much that means to ole Daisy."

"Hey," said April, "Are we gonna sit her all night jawing or are we going to bed?"

She and Daisy got up, hugged each other and started to bed. After they both checked on J.J. and made sure he was secure for the night, they parted. Both had a good feeling inside them.

15

MOVING FORWARD

April had her baby boy and he was the spitting image of Jason. Again Jason strutted like a cock rooster. April told him that they should wait at least a few years and try for a little girl. The delivery was quick and she suffered no consequences. J.J. was quite receptive to the new baby, thanks to Penelope's presence. They decided to call him Jeremy after his father. It broke April's heart that this son, Jason's real son, couldn't be Junior. At least the boys would share the same initials.

The lawyer managed to arrange a buy on several houses that April wanted. There was a major drive put on other landlords in the area to improve their properties. If they didn't, stiff penalties were levied against them.

Claudette had completed the work for her GED and was enrolled in child care classes. April had helped her obtain a license to set up a nursery and day care center in one of these old homes. Everything was legal. Claudette had a low interest loan and now could have a decent place to live as well as a steady income. She had put on a little weight and didn't look so gaunt. She and April were steadfast friends who felt comfortable in discussing any subject that came up in a conversation. The young girl had her confidence back and proved this time and time again in the level headed decisions needing to be made for the business to run smoothly. Her interviews of workers were thorough and she insisted that if they worked hard, their benefits would increase. Above all, they must be honest and love children.

April tried to spend more time with J.J. and Jeremy but it seemed everyone wanted some of her precious time. She was on so many committees and attended so many luncheons and events that she felt her whole life was spent changing clothes and running back and forth from one meeting to another.

J.J. would soon start kindergarten and Jeremy was into everything when April discovered that she was pregnant again. Little Jennifer was born without fan fare. She was truly a beauty. Jason was fulfilled. Throughout the years it seemed that their marriage had grown better and their love making was constantly improving, if that was possible.

Jason's mother had died before little Jennifer was born so she never got to see her granddaughter. However, there was a trust fund established for her as well as the boys in accordance with her will. Each child was rich beyond their wildest dreams. All they had to do was grow up to inherit.

Daisy had adamantly refused retirement so she was still in charge of the children. They adored her. Little Jennifer had her wound around her finger from the cradle.

Jason's position grew stronger as he was asked to take charge of more important committees. He was now the senior Senator from Georgia and Speaker of the house. April loved to tease him and say that she was glad he was employed because they had a house full of hungry children. A year later little Janet joined the family. By this time, April told Jason that she thought they should seriously consider using birth control. At this rate, they would be having babies until they were both gray and on social security. He would just smile and say that he would love a hundred if they were a product of his and her love. Anyway, it was fun making them. Surely Betty didn't want to stop practicing. She kissed him and agreed that she did not.

Jason had completed his fourth term in the Senate and the children had developed nicely. They were not sent to private schools. April insisted they go through the public system unless they ran into learning problems. They would not grow up in a protected bubble like their father had. Their schools were integrated and they rode the bus like hundreds of other children.

Jason came home early one afternoon and said that he had been approached and asked how he felt about being nominated for Vice President of the United States?

April smiled and said, "It's about time them boys on the hill recognized real talent."

Jason hugged her and kissed her passionately. Since Daisy was napping and the children were in school, they ran up the staircase to the bedroom and spent hours making love. Their lives were so full, thought April. It seemed that the world was theirs for the taking. She had been using a contraceptive cream though. If Jason ran for Vice President, she didn't want to be left behind. Surely four children was enough.

That evening the news reported that the candidates being considered for Vice Presidency were Jason Stewart and Max Hartley. The commentator went on about their accomplishments and what committees they served on, etc. etc.

April could not believe that Max had been asked to run for the same office as Jason. After all, Jason was far more experienced. Oh well, she would just wait for the nominations to be confirmed.

Realizing that visibility was necessary to reinforce Jason's nomination, she pitched in like a woman possessed. Jason had worked so hard for this position, he deserved to win, she thought.

Fate is something that no one can explain. Why it happens, when it happens, or for what reason. It can be good or it can be bad. Fate was the key player in events leading up to the selection of the Vice President.

April still could not believe her ears when she heard that Serena and her two daughters were killed this evening when their car was struck by a dump truck on the George Washington Parkway. Her heart was heavy. Poor Max, to be denied his son was bad enough. But to lose both his wife and both his children was too much.

Jason insisted that he and Betty give Max as much support as possible throughout this trying period. Max became a frequent fixture around their house. Jason was aware that there was something between these two but he just couldn't put his finger on it. Betty was always polite, but she never encouraged these visits. Max was so attached to the two Stewart boys that he was always coming around wanting to take them somewhere. J.J. worshipped him. Secretly April wanted to tell him that J.J. was his own flesh and blood but she would not. She owed Jason all her loyalty. Besides, she did not know how Max would react if he learned this secret. She was still bitter about him telling her that she could have jeopardized his career by becoming pregnant in the first place.

Several times, when Max had taken J.J. and Jeremy to a hockey game or to see the Washington Senator's play, people had told him what a handsome son he had. When Max explained that J.J. was Senator Stewart's son, they were taken back. He certainly looks enough like you to be your son, they would state. This bothered Max more than he cared to admit. There was no doubt that he would be proud to have this kid as his own.

Whenever April heard this remark, her heart turned to ice. She would have to do something to keep these two apart. What if Max pushed an investigation into the crash and found out that she was April Simmons, not Betty Stewart. This news would destroy Jason. He worshiped his older son. He couldn't love J.J. more if he were his own flesh and blood. Her life would be over. She had managed to keep this secret for fourteen years, it couldn't come out now. Oh God, she prayed, not now.

For the first time in her life, April suggested to Jason that he thought J.J. and Jeremy should go to a private school. They would be better prepared for college and would learn discipline away from home. The exposure would be good for them. Jason was surprised. All these years Betty had fought against private schools. Well, she had been right about the children so far, so if this was what she wanted, so be it. He would not prevent it.

An excellent school was selected in Georgia. April's heart almost broke when she saw the boys off. She would miss them dearly. They had been such a close and happy family. However, she felt threatened and sought to protect her son at all costs. Max was devastated when he found out the boys had been shipped off to Georgia. April found out later that J.J. had called Max in tears asking if he couldn't help get him and Jeremy returned to Maryland. Max felt so helpless. His social life had decreased considerably now that the boys were gone. He had enjoyed taking them to sports activities and to the zoo. Why on earth Betty Stewart had decided to ship them off now was a real mystery to him. Guess it had to do with the up coming election.

Max was flattered about being nominated for Vice President. Only eight years ago he was happy being chosen as the Senator from Missouri. Politics had been good to him. No one in Washington knew how miserable his life with Serena had been. She was always putting on her social grace when they were out in public. At home she was a prize bitch. He had loved his children though and for them, they decided to continue the charade of a happy couple on Capitol Hill. Serena was always politically minded.

He found himself remembering more and more the pure love he had shared with a young girl named April. She would never know how badly he felt when he turned her away. Serena was so beautiful. He was totally bewitched with her beauty and her father's political connections. She had helped his career beyond even their expectations and he was grateful for that. But Serena was no April when it came to loving. She was a cold selfish bitch. He found this out on their wedding night and things never got any better. Serena chose to get pregnant because her father needed an heir. Preferably a grandson, to leave his wealth to. They both got cheated in the deal, he thought. His daughters were beautiful and loving, but under Serena's influence, he saw they would grow up cold and calculating just like her. How he ached for a son. Many times he had wondered about the child that had died in the crash. Could it have been the son he would never know?

16

SEEKING THE TRUTH

Max was possessed with the thought that J.J. Stewart could be his child. He began his search for proof. First, he went back to the manifest of the aircraft. Betty Stewart and April had been seated side by side according to the records. Could Betty have switched seats with April? Hadn't everyone mistaken J.J. Stewart for his son? Max set out to try and discover if this possibility, no matter how remote, could have happened. He became obsessed with the thought.

He started with the archives at the hospital. There he pulled the records of Betty Stewart. Her face was truly a mess according to the old pictures on file. Her teeth were gone, jaw and nose broken, burns all over her face. There were absolutely no clues in the pictures. Max was not a medical person, but he studied the X-rays intently. There had been severe movement of the jaw and some carving down of the cheek bones. April had had high cheek bones. The lips had been scarred and reshaped. The files were absolutely useless. The only alternative was to approach Betty Stewart.

Max called the school where J.J. and Jeremy were enrolled and stated that he was going to be in the area and would like for the boys to join him for a late dinner before returning to Washington. The schoolmaster promised to arrange it.

The flight was slow. Thank God there was a major airport in Atlanta. Max couldn't wait to see J.J. again. The very thought of this child being his caused him great joy and anxiety.

Max rented a car and drove to the school. While he was waiting for the boys to be paged, he asked the office attendant if the records showed the boys blood type. The administrator said he would pull the records and verify the types. He was told that J.J.'s blood was O Positive and Jeremy's was A Positive.

Max's heart soared. J.J. had the same blood type as he did. He knew that Betty was A positive from the hospital records. He had checked the Senate's records and discovered that Jason was also A positive.

As the boys entered the room, he was once again thrilled and puzzled by the face of the older boy. A clone could not have been a more perfect match than this child. He knew in his heart that J.J. Stewart was his child. April was alive and posing as Betty Stewart. Was she so desperate when she fled Missouri? How had she managed to fool so many people for such a long time? She and Jason would be celebrating their twentieth anniversary soon. Well he had to admit that she had fooled him and he had known her as Betty Stewart for over fifteen years.

That evening as Max was flying back to Washington, April received a call from the boys. They were so happy that Uncle Max had stopped over to see him. He had taken them to an expensive restaurant and to a show.

April tried her best to keep her voice level. "That's wonderful darling," she said. "I will have your father thank him tomorrow at work."

Inside April was seething. That Bastard! After all these years and now when a nomination for Vice Presidency was on the line, Max was digging up the past. April was sitting in the dark when Jason came into the room. Kissing her on the forehead he asked, "Darling, is something wrong?"

"No dear, everything is fine. The boys just called and said Max stopped in and took them to dinner and a show tonight."

"Well now that was nice of him," said Jason. "I'll be sure to thank him tomorrow at work."

"Yes you do that," said April.

All night long April tossed and turned. How could he have found out, she wondered. Was it something I said or did that gave me away? She saw her life ending. Jason would leave her. He would take her children and leave her with nothing but shame. She had worked so hard to help his career. His career would probably end. Oh dear God, please help me now she prayed. She loved this man laying beside her.

Jason noticed that Betty was jumpy and edgy lately. She had lost weight and was steadily declining dinner invitations. Anytime he mentioned Max Hartley's name, she cringed. That man had done something to his wife and he intended to find out what it was.

Max returned to Washington more convinced now than ever before in his life that he had a son. He was so happy. He knew it would hurt some people when he revealed the news, but his having a son would out weigh the hurt.

Serena had not wanted children at all but she decided that in order to keep her father's wealth, she must have an heir. When the first child was a girl, they tried again. After the second girl she was so angry and blamed Max. She refused to have sex with him again unless he had a vasectomy. He had done this quietly as he had no way of knowing that a freak accident would claim Serena, but his two lovely daughters also. Now he was alone. Not if I can prove that J.J. Stewart is my child, he thought. Why hadn't he had the foresight to marry April when he had the chance? Why had he thrown away a life that he saw was almost perfect with one of his colleagues. That family could have been his.

Max picked up the telephone many times to call Betty Stewart and arrange a meeting. What could he do if she denied everything he wanted to hear? He couldn't go to the press. He couldn't go to Jason. Jason would probably beat the hell out of him if he even mentioned that his wife was less than perfect. And he worshiped J.J. The older son had some special place in the web of their lives and it was obvious to outsiders.

Weeks passed and Max became anxious. How could he approach Betty Stewart or April?

One afternoon while the Senate was in recess, he got into his car and drove out to the Stewart's in Bethesda. Betty was in the garden pruning flowers and was wearing cutoff jeans and one of Jason's big shirts. A floppy hat covered her blond hair that was beginning to be streaked with gray.

When she saw him, she froze. Being the elegant lady that she was though, she walked toward him and extended her hand. There was a frozen smile on her face. "What brings you out this way this time of day," she asked?

April saw the bags under his eyes and the loose skin on his jaws. He looked ten years older than he did when she had seen him last month. Max saw similar symptoms in April's face. "Please give me just a minute to talk to you in private. I need to talk to you. First I know that you are not Betty Stewart. You switched seats with Betty Stewart on that airplane and April, you have been masquerading as Betty Stewart. Believe me, I don't want to hurt you. I just want to claim my rightful heir. J.J. is my son please tell me that he is my son."

A cry escaped April's lips. "Max Hartley have you gone mad? What a preposterous story if every I heard one. Dear man, I suggest that you get medical assistance before you lose all your senses."

"April," he cried. "April please I am so alone and so lonely. Serena was such a bitch and made my life a living hell. Now that she and both of my daughters are gone, I have no one. I can't have anymore children because I had a vasectomy. Please I don't want to hurt you, but I need to know the truth. I want to hear you say that J.J. is my son. Not Jason's son, my son."

April was furious. 'Get out of my house, and stay away from my children. If you ever come back here I will have you arrested. I have heard that this town causes decent people to act crazy, but this is the cheapest trick I have ever encountered to keep a man from being elected to a political office. I believe that you would pull down a fine honest person like Jason Stewart just so you could win the nomination over him. You are despicable. Leave now and don't ever speak to me or my family again. If you approach my sons again, I will have you arrested. You have totally flipped Senator."

April stormed into the house. Daisy had been sitting outside beside a hedge dividing the garden where April had been working. She heard the whole conversation. Tears rolled down her face. What she had suspected for years was now spoken in the open. Betty Stewart was never and could never have become this woman that had made Jason so happy. No wonder she had come home so changed. The Betty upstairs was and would always be Betty Stewart to Daisy in her heart. That chile had had a rough time. Imagine that man throwing her over when he discovered she was pregnant and marrying another woman. Served him right, she though. If his life was a living hell, he deserved it. Daisy would die with this secret in her heart.

Daisy had to admit that J.J. did look more like Max Hartley than he should. There was no doubt in her mind that J.J. was Max's child.

Jason came home late that evening. Betty seemed more subdued than usual. "Darling, why don't you and Daisy fly down to Atlanta and visit the boys? The trip would be good for both of you."

April looked at Jason. She loved this man with every inch of her being. To lose him now would be a death sentence to her. Would she lose him if she told him the truth? She couldn't take the chance.

Trying to keep her voice normal she said. "Jason, Max came by here today with a drummed up story that caused me to ask him to leave and never come back. You know how he has been since that accident that took Serena and the girls. Well, I think he has flipped out or is sincerely trying to create some situation that would cause you to lose the election."

"Betty," said Jason, "What on earth are you talking about. What could Max possibly do to make you so angry. I have always sensed that you did not like the man, but to throw him out of our house! What on earth did he do?"

"He came by here today and accused me of being the girl that died next to me on the airplane. He said that girl was pregnant with his child and that I was that girl and J.J. is his son."

"Jason exploded! That bastard said what? I will kill him with my bare hands. How dare he. Oh darling, I will take care of this in my own way."

April ran to Jason and let him hold her close. She was crying hysterically. Thank God he loved her enough not to question any of what she had just told him. That proved that Jason loved her too.

Sleep was impossible that night. April kept seeing Max's face. She had actually felt sorry for him. Her instinct to protect her child and her husband had been stronger though and she hoped she had convinced Jason that Max was ill. She would always wonder if Max would leave it alone now or continue his pursuit in trying to unravel this mess. Her guard must always be up.

Max had gone to his personal physical and asked if it were possible for two people who had "A" positive blood to have a child with blood type "O". The doctor had stated that "O" was a universal donor type that could be compatible with "A". It was unusual, but not impossible.

17

THE CONFRONTATION

Jason stormed into Max's office. His face was bright red and it was obvious that he was angry. He walked over to the desk and said very loudly, "How dare you go to my house and accuse my wife of adultery, among other things. I have a restraining order to keep you away from my home, my wife, and my children. Don't ever approach them again or I will beat your ass to a pulp. If anyone ever told me that you would stoop to such outrageous political dirty tricks, I would not have believed it."

"Jason," said Max. "I know you are upset, but if you will just hear me out. This has nothing to do with our political careers."

Jason interrupted, saying. "I can assure you sir that I have no interest in anything you will ever say again. Keep your distance from me and don't ever attempt to approach any member of my family again as long as you live." Having said this, Jason stormed out of Max's office. He was so angry he felt like tearing it from the hinges.

When he got to his own office, he sat down and looked out the window. Now that he was over his anger, he thought about what Max had said. Betty certainly was different after the plane crash. She was more loving, more involved, and certainly family oriented. The woman he had lived with before was cold, selfish and was more interested in being a Senator's wife than being a wife. She had insisted on separate bedrooms. And, as much as he adored his older son, he had to admit, J.J. was the spitting image of Max. He had never noticed this before.

Sitting there, tears ran down Jason's face. Was it possible? He remembered the words Betty had uttered in Macon when they were campaigning. She had cried out that this child was Jason's child, God, don't let her lose Jason's child. All the pieces were there, he had just never looked at the complete puzzle before.

This would explain her concerns about civil rights. Even her dress had changed from tailored to more feminine. Was it possible?

Jason sat for hours pondering the situation. What was he to do? He and Betty or April, whoever she was, could not continue their lives as they had in the past. God, he thought, I could kill Max Hartley. Why did he have to mess up the most wonderful thing in my life?

If this woman was April Simmons, as Max suggested, that meant his wife was dead. Somehow, Jason could not comprehend this. His life had more meaning and fulfillment since the crash. How could he grieve for a situation that had only gotten better?

What was he to do? When it was time to go home, Jason did not know how to approach Betty. He had serious doubts, even though she had denied Max's claim. Betty had never lied to him before. Again, he thought, was she so desperate to protect a child, and would she go to this length to continue it? He and Betty were soon to celebrate twenty years of married life. Sixteen of those years were with an impostor. Jason was clearly puzzled. Still in his mind he knew that he loved his wife, whoever she is. And, he adored his family.

The real hurt was wondering if the son had wanted so long and so badly that had been nurtured through the years, was really his child or Max Hartley's son. Jason loved this child with such depth that even the other children realized the bond between them was one they could never enter.

Jason decided that he had to face this situation. He would go home, talk to Betty and surely after all they had been through together, they would work this out. Whoever she was, he had loved her this long, that could not be put aside so casually. Could he forgive her? He honestly didn't know. This was something they would both have to work at.

18

THE ACCIDENT

April had been sitting on the patio for hours without speaking to anyone. The children were sent to the playroom and Daisy was allowing her all the space she needed to think things through. Daisy's heart was breaking seeing how Max raising the issue of Betty's identity had changed the whole family. Jason was polite, but distant. Betty just sat and stared into space.

When Jason arrived he found Betty on the porch. "Darling, we need to talk. First I want to tell you that I sincerely love you. The issue raised by Max is unfortunate but there are certain things that I just don't understand. When you denied his claim, I believed you. Help me darling, help me believe it now. Make this easy for both of us and let's get to the truth of the matter. Living like this is harming the girls and the tension between us is something I do not like. Please, Betty, help me work through this."

April looked at Jason. He looked so sincere yet pathetic. Would she lose him if she told him the truth? All these years they had lived a lie and had been so happy. It wasn't just J.J.'s life at stake now, it was all her children. They were all hers and she loved them all. What would Max and Jason do if she told them that J.J. was indeed Max's son? How would this information affect J.J.? He worshiped Jason.

When she could find her voice, she spoke so softly that the words seemed to be coming from a far away place.

"Jason, I am your wife. J.J. is our son. Max Hartley wants so badly to have an heir that he is trying to use the one thing he knows you treasure more than life to upset you in the election. What he has told you about me and our son, I don't care to know. If you wish to believe him and doubt me, I'm sorry for you. We need to put this aside and get on with our lives. Our family needs us and Jason, I need you. I need you to love me without looking at me to see if I am different than I was before Max came by last week. If we have problems, we can work them out. Through the years we have jumped many hurdles and always came out of it together. I ask you now to put this issue aside and let me be your loving wife again."

Jason let her put her arms around him. The very smell of her perfume and the feel of her touch was magnetic. He looked longingly at her. At this very moment he knew that what she said was true. He kissed her tenderly and they walked arm and arm to the bedroom. Once again they made love and held each other tenderly all through the night. Neither wanted to let go. However, the seed of suspicion had been planted and April was to see a look on Jason's face from time to time that indicated to her that he still had doubts.

April began to make plans for the holidays. The boys would be returning to Bethesda for the family celebrations. She was so anxious to see them. Silently she prayed that Max would not interfere and spoil everything for them.

The boys had grown so tall and they were both so very handsome. April felt that she could just smother them with kisses and hugs every minute they were around. Jason spent as much time as he could at home.

Again, it was obvious that he singled J.J. out and listened intently to every word the boy spoke. He decided that parenthood was not an issue in his feelings for this child. His birth had brought a mild marriage together and made it blissful. His feelings were as strong as they had ever been. To hell with Max Hartley, he thought.

J.J. had asked if Uncle Max would be stopping by later. He and Jeremy would love to see him. It was really too bad that he had to spend the holidays alone wasn't it? If this was a hint, both Jason and April chose to ignore it. Jason mumbled something about Max going home to Missouri for the holidays. Maybe next year.

Jeremy asked April if he had to return to school in Georgia. He really hated it. Being J.J.'s little brother was a real pain. J.J. did everything first and better. He loved J.J. but would prefer to stay home and attend school in Bethesda if it was permitted. April promised to talk to Jason about it later. Jeremy was growing up so quick. It broke her heart to be parted from them. Had she been right in sending them away. She didn't know?

After they finished their lunch Jason had taken J.J. out in the car. He wanted to get a license soon. It was hard to believe he was almost sixteen. Jeremy just sulked around the house. He had been asked to go, but decided not to. Even when he was around his dad and J.J., they seemed to ignore him. He got more attention from his mom.

April, Daisy, Jeremy and the girls were playing crazy eight when the doorbell rang. Daisy came running back to the den yelling and screaming. "Miss Betty come quick! There's been an accident and the police are here."

April thought she would die. The policeman said that the Senator and his son had been involved in a car accident and been taken to Bethesda Naval Hospital. April thanked the policeman and rang for John.

Daisy stayed with the children. Jeremy grabbed his jacket and accompanied April to the hospital. He was almost fifteen so he should be allowed to visit. Besides, he wanted to be there for his mom.

John had talked with the police officers while others were telling April about the accident. J.J. had been driving and tried to over correct when he hit a patch of ice. He lost control of the car and ran head on into a telephone pole. The car had caught fire but several people had witnessed it and been there to pull the two people out.

April thought she had faced every crisis possible in her life up to this point. She had overcome so many obstacles to get to where she was now. Oh God, please don't let Jason and my baby die. Take me instead, but don't harm them for my mistakes. Jeremy saw his mom was crying and put his arm around her. "Mom, everything is going to be okay. Dad is tough and J.J. is indestructible. I know. He always comes out on top no what the cause or how many odds. He's a born winner."

April squeezed Jeremy's hand. He was so good and gentle like his father. She was glad he had come along with her.

Finally the doctor came out and told April that Jason had internal bleeding and would need emergency surgery. His spleen would have to be removed and there were several broken bones. These could be set, but the major problem was the contusion on his head. He had been cut just above the eye and the glass had intruded inside the head. Whether it had pierced the brain yet, they didn't know. He had not regained consciousness and they had no way of knowing if he had brain damage or not. His eyes and reflex were totally unresponsive. If she would give permission, they would start immediately to restore him.

The boy was pinned under the steering wheel and the steering column had snapped and impaled him. He was alive but was critical. The rescue people had done a good job of getting him out of the car, but there had been so much bleeding. They were checking now to see if his heart and lungs had been spared. A surgical team was being assembled. With her permission, they would begin.

April thought that God, who had been so good to her, surely couldn't be punishing her this much for her sins. Dear God, she could not lose either of them. Here life without her husband and son would be unbearable. She had tried to protect J.J. so much. Had she done the right thing?

Jeremy was a rock. April refused to leave the hospital. Coffee and sandwiches were brought to her and Jeremy. He forced her to eat to keep up her strength.

He was like a pit bull watching over her. She saw strength in him that made her proud. He was always such a sweet and gentle child. It felt good to know that he was standing strong beside her.

The doctors had worked through most of the night and around midnight one brought April the news. "Mrs. Stewart, I hate to bring you bad news, but your son died on the operating table half an hour ago. He was just torn up too badly to put back together."

April felt as if she had been cast off the earth and was floating in outer space somewhere. She heard a voice saying, "Mother I am here. Come back to me. I need you." Jeremy was hugging her and crying silently as he begged her to come back to him. He thought that she had left him too as he watched the expression on her face. It was as if she stopped living and was suspended somewhere he could not go. She opened her eyes and said. "Darling, I am here. You know that J.J. has left us. It's going to be rough going on without him. Smiling through her tears, she said. "Thank God I still have you."

It was early morning before she got word about Jason. He was out of surgery but he wasn't out of trouble. They suggested that Mrs. Stewart go home and rest as the Senator would be sedated for hours to come. They promised to call if there was any change.

Jeremy called John and had him come for him and his mom. The loss of J.J. was going to be really rough on her. He couldn't imagine what it would do to his father. J.J. was his favorite. If Jason survived the trauma of the accident, finding out about J.J. would probably kill him.

Daisy was waiting. She and April clung to each other and cried until there were no more tears. Jeremy called his sisters together and told them that J.J. had been hurt in a car accident and that he was now in Heaven. Tenderly he helped them back to bed. He told them to be quiet because mom was sad and needed to rest. If they needed anything, they were to call on him or Daisy.

After Jeremy was sure his mom was in bed and had fallen asleep, he went in and sat beside her bed. When she called out, he took her hand until he too fell asleep.

When April woke, she saw him sitting there. He was so young but he had proven that he was tough. The boy had great strength that was hidden behind his gentle nature.

Carefully she kissed Jeremy and helped him to his bedroom. The child was exhausted. She was amazed at how well he was handling his grief. He and J.J. had been inseparable. J.J. was a leader, but Jeremy didn't seem to mind. He just joined in and went along.

April got up, took a bath, dressed and told Daisy that she was going back to the hospital. She wanted to be there when Jason woke up. Jeremy would sleep for a while. She left word with Daisy that if he wanted to join her at the hospital later, it was okay. Just make sure he eats a good meal before he comes.

Jason's private room was full of life saving equipment. The hiss and clicks of the machinery was enough to make one scream. Jason looked so small and pale laying there against the white sheets. Some sixteen years ago, he had stood beside her in a room similar to this. Waiting patiently for her to wake up, as she was doing now. How, she thought, am I going to tell him about J.J.?

Days went by and Jason lay in a coma. April read to him, talked to him and held his hand. She had said so many prayers. He just had to pull through. Would all this have happened if she had told him the truth? It was obvious that he treated J.J. with the same loving care he had always shown before Max tried to destroy their family. If he ever doubted the child's birthright, it was not visible in his actions over the holidays.

April was dozing when she felt someone's presence in the room. When she looked up and saw Max Hartley, her first reaction was one of hatred. Before she could speak, he said. "Betty I heard about the accident and I know that J.J. is dead. If there is anything I can do to assist you and your family right now or in the future, just let me know. I truly loved that boy like a son. The time we spent together was wonderful and I enjoyed it more than you can ever know. Whether he was mine or not, he was a wonderful boy. Please find it in your heart to let me be your friend and help you through this awful period in your life."

After he had said this, he walked over and hugged April. She was too exhausted to fight. His son was dead. The least she could do was include him in the arrangements. J.J. was gone. There was nothing left to fight over.

J.J.'s body was flown to Atlanta and placed in the family plot. She had contacted the Millers and used the services of the Higgins Funeral Home. They were very happy to help her through her grief. She had given them their dignity years ago, it was the least they could do. They told her that they were making a profitable business out of the place and making sure no one got cheated. Ole Higgins had found out early on that Rufus and Bo were managing and his role was that of a front man. It had been difficult in the beginning when he found out that his partners were black, but he came through.

Jason was still in a coma and knew nothing of the events taking place around him. Max had flown with the Stewart family to Georgia and was very helpful in making the arrangements. The funeral was splendid but tasteful.

The trip back to Washington was long and tiring. The girls were subdued and Jeremy was trying his best to interest them in some games. This child was a real treasure. He had not openly displayed his grief, but April knew he was dealing with it. She would not interfere. Even if he had been envious of J.J., April knew that he loved and admired his brother. She made a mental note to talk to him about his feelings when they got home.

The following morning April returned to the hospital. When she walked into his room, he was so still that she thought he was still in a coma. As she bent down to kiss him, he opened his eyes. "Darling, how are you," he asked? "I woke up and you weren't here. I got really scared. But your here now, that's all that matters."

April had tears in her eyes. Jason was still talking. He was going to be all right. "Ole J.J. was driving that car like a real pro," he was saying. "Then he hit some ice and...Betty, I don't remember what happened after that? Is he okay? What happened to me? Why am I here?"

Gently April took Jason's hand. "J.J. over corrected and lost control of the car. You and he tore up a telephone pole on Rockville Pike. You were hit on the head and J.J. was pinned in the car. They got him out darling, but it was too late."

Jason was trying to make sense of what Betty was saying. "You mean J.J. is dead!"

"Yes darling, I am afraid so. You have been in a coma for almost two weeks. The family flew to Georgia and had J.J. placed in the family plot. We just got back yesterday."

"Betty, I loved that boy. I'm so sorry I ever doubted you. He knew that he was loved and that he was special. Having him brought you and me back together, didn't it? Now that he's gone, are you going to stay with me?"

"Jason, how on earth could you even ask? I love you darling. If possible, a little more each day. Please get well and come home to me. I need you Jason. I need your strength and your love. The family needs you too."

The doctor came in and seeing Betty, said hello. He told her that Jason still had some swelling in the brain area but from the EEG and neurological tests there didn't seem to be any permanent damage. He had a broken leg that had to have a pin inserted in it and several broken ribs. If she promised not to take him dancing for a couple of months, he could be released in a couple of days and keep in touch through the out patient clinic.

Betty thanked the doctor and sat down by the bed. "Jason, you are coming home. I feel that now is the time to tell you that Jeremy doesn't want to return to school in Georgia. Considering the circumstances I think I would like to have him home. What do you think?"

"Darling, I never want to be separated from you or the kids again as long as I live. Let's get back to where we were a year ago. We can do it Betty. Seems we both come from pretty sturdy stock. Let's start today putting bad things behind us and walk through the future together."

April went home that night and thanked God for such a wonderful person. She had been spared again.

19

REBUILDING

They continued their lives as if Max Hartley's claims had never happened. Their love life improved even more than before and once again April found herself pregnant. Jason was as happy about this pregnancy as he was about all the others. Whether God was punishing April or she had reached the age where she could no longer have healthy pregnancies she wasn't sure but the miscarriage was a big disappointment to the whole family.

Jason soon returned to work. He won the nomination for Vice President and April became more and more involved in volunteer work. Her "father's" small fortune allowed her to help many unfortunates. Mostly she assisted individuals who were brought to her attention by well meaning friends or was contacted through the social services agencies.

April now had six houses on East Capitol Street, fully renovated and six proud families living in them. This was a wonderful opportunity for them to own their own home and to get such low interest rates. There seemed to be a sense of pride on the street now. She still maintained a good relationship with the mayor and other officials involved with forcing landlords throughout the city to keep their properties in good order. If there were discrepancies found and were not immediately acted upon, they were heavily fined and taken to court.

Another of April's issues was helping social services find decent foster homes and mothers. She visited the wards of the military hospitals and took gifts of robes, house slippers, combs, toothpaste and books. She even paid dependent's fares and motel bills if a family member had an extended stay. At the VA Hospitals she always hired a barber to come in and give free haircuts to those who wanted them. She bought up blocks of tickets to the Hockey Games and to the football games. These were passed out generously to the military members who were selected for outstanding accomplishments.

Through her contacts with the Navy relief she was informed of really needy people who did not qualify for loans or gratuities. She was always ready and willing to furnish rides for elderly people, making sure they got to and from their doctor's appointments. Her daughters assisted these older people with their shopping and would read the newspapers and books to them.

Jeremy had taken to shopping off at Jason's office every evening after school and just helping out however he could. He would run errands, file, empty trash, Xerox, whatever anyone needed done, he was willing to do. No job was too menial for him. Secretly he hoped that his father would transfer the love he had given so unselfishly to J.J. to him. They were close and Jeremy knew his father loved him, but he had always been envious of the relationship J.J. had with his dad. Even in death, J.J. still held a special place in Jason's heart.

April was currently campaigning for better health and child care for working mothers. Again she had used her own private wealth to establish several clinics and lobbied for assistance for facilities to train young under privileged women to gain GED's and enroll in college courses. She tried her best to convince Jason that women needed more rights and that Congress should introduce bills in support of these rights.

Jeremy was very interested in his mother's political views and assisted her whenever possible. He had recently been given an unofficial appointment in the office of the new Congressman from Georgia. His manner was not as outgoing as J.J.'s had been, but those who took the time to know him recognized the strength concealed underneath the good looks, excellent manners, and intelligent face.

Max was welcomed again into the Stewart's home. April had told Jason how Max had assisted her during the ordeal of J.J.'s funeral. If there were ill feelings, they were deeply hidden by all.

Being the Vice President's wife was one of much social involvement. April rose to the challenge easily and won the hearts of all. She listened patiently to all problems brought to her and sought realistic and workable solutions. She was involved with the District Government as well as the Federal Government. Her campaign for human rights was known throughout the country. Someone had written about how she had helped families who needed support as well as financial aid and how she had willingly assisted them. Jason remarked several times that maybe she would have to run for office. She was better known than he was.

April wondered where the office of the Vice President would take them. Would Jason seek the Presidency or had he had enough political life?

They hadn't talked about the future recently and it bothered her. He would be an excellent choice, she thought.

Fate again intervened. The President was attending the Army/Navy Game in Annapolis when he was shot and killed by a sniper. Jason was only grazed on the arm, but he became President instantly. There was only nine months remaining of the President's term. April never saw enough of her husband during this time. She was concerned when she saw how much he had aged in such a short time.

Jason's name was entered as a candidate for President and he chose as his running mate, Senator Max Hartley from the grand State of Missouri. Max had worked along side Jason on so many projects. Their friendship had been reinstated and they were an excellent pair of politicians to carry the great Country forward.

April enjoyed moving into the White House but she missed her own beautiful house in Bethesda. Daisy said she was too tired to move again. The children were too big to need her anymore. She just stayed on in the house in Bethesda. April employed a staff to watch over her old friend. The children would often ride out on the weekend and visit her. No one was more loved than Daisy. She was as much a part of the Stewart family as the children themselves. And, she knew it.

It was during this time that April received a letter in the mail with no return address. It was poorly typed stating that they knew her secret. She immediately approached Jason. The letter was turned over to the Secret Service. Once again April became apprehensive and feared exposure.

Jason told her to ignore the letter and pretend it didn't happen. Yet, whether it was her own paranoia or just what, she thought Jason was looking at her in a different way lately. God, why did this have to happen now? Was it an angry politician? Was this a ploy to discredit both Jason and Max? What puzzled her most was what did they mean by "her secret?" Did they know that she wasn't Betty Stewart or did they know that J.J. was not Jason's son? Which secret did they know, what would the press do with this information? How badly would this hurt Jason in the upcoming election?

April became so upset that she suggested to Jason that she fly out to Boulder to assist Mrs. Baker with fund raising for the safe house that had been established in her father's home. She would not like a lot of press. Because she was the wife of the President, she couldn't just fly off on a commercial flight. No, because they had accepted the political life, they had to accept the disadvantages that came with it. April hated having bodyguards around all the time and rarely got to drive herself anywhere. Everything she or her family did was public. The children found it a bother in the beginning but had since adjusted far better than April ever could.

When she arrived in Boulder, Sam Carpenter met her plane. April was not sure who this person was, but she greeted him cordially. He accompanied her entourage to the safe house. After April had greeted everyone and shook everyone's hand, she was getting a soda when Sam Carpenter approached her again.

"Betty, you act like you don't remember me. Don't you remember the prom we went to when you were in High School? Better still, how could you just shut me out of your life when you returned to Washington? Didn't you tell me how comfortable you were with me when we went dancing night after night. Can you just forget those intimate dinners? How you were considering a divorce. The passionate encounters we had in and around Boulder as well as my last "secret" visit to D.C.? That baby you were carrying is probably mine."

April turned to stare at this man. How dare he. So what if Betty had been lonely and sought an old friends companionship? What on earth was this man driving at?

Not wanting to be bothered anymore, April simply walked back into the crowd. She could see that she had dented this maniac's ego. However one thing was for sure. She did not want to encourage this man. Even in her wildest dreams, April would never have suspected Betty of infidelity. Was he lying?

Staying as long as possible at the fund raising event, April became apprehensive when it was time to return to her hotel. She didn't want to confide in the Secret Service that she was afraid of this person. What if they arrested him and the paper got wind of the whole thing. If he was so bold as to approach April in a public place, he would gladly give some wild story to the media. What on earth did he want? Was he the person who sent the letter to the White House?

April could not sleep. Sam Carpenter was not the type of person that could be put off easily. Perhaps it would be better if she met with him and found out just what he wanted. Surely the media couldn't make a scandal out of two old high school friends having lunch in a public place, or could they?

My God, she thought, I am no longer the sexy young woman he remembers. What in the world does he want with a middle aged woman with four children?

Well, she would meet him if he persisted and made contact with her again. If not, she would promptly forget the encounter.

Jason called and April was again calmed. Deception or not, Betty could never have loved this man the way April loved him. She always prayed for Betty but thanked God in the same breath for her good fortune. The plane crash had allowed her a life she would never have dreamed possible.

Sam Carpenter did not try to approach April again while she was in Boulder, so she flew back to Washington. She was glad to be home. The children had missed her and she them.

The whole family decided to spend Christmas in the house in Bethesda with Daisy. Betty had no living family and since Jason's mother had died, there was no reason to return to Georgia this year to celebrate the holidays. It would be fun to return to the house they all loved so well and sit and talk to Daisy. Whether she wanted it or not, Daisy found herself on the receiving end of being taken care of. The children anticipated her every need and could never do enough for her. Max was invited also. April was surprised, but delighted, when he declined. He had recently met some young lobbyist and was going to spend the holiday with her. They were going to Aspen to ski. This news made April happier than she realized. He needed someone in his life. It would be a shame for him to grow old and bitter in his old age.

Politics was his first love now, but maybe if this person was special enough, all this would change.

April and Jason gave Jeremy his first car that Christmas. It was tough for him to have the secret service follow him everywhere though. Just when he though he was ready for some privacy, his dad becomes President and he has to have baby-sitters.

The whole family got in the Christmas spirit and there was a lot of hushed conversations when someone entered a room. April feared opening closets in the event she would find some secret treasure that one of the children had put away to wrap for that special morning.

On Christmas Eve, April received another letter. Again it had no return address, no signature, but had the same message. "I know your secret."

Because of the long awaited holiday, April decided not to show the letter to anyone. She tried to put this troublesome disturbance out of her mind. After all, Jason would have the entire day to spend with the whole family tomorrow. How they still enjoyed quality time they spent together as a family. Young Jennifer and Janet were getting new clothing. They were really into clothes at this point of their lives.

Christmas was everything the glorious event should be. There were a few awkward moments when J.J. was mentioned. His presence was sorely missed.

The following morning before Jason returned to the White House, April asked if he would send one of his most trusted Secret Service agents by the house. She showed Jason the second letter and told him she had received it on Christmas Eve. Jason was gravely concerned.

Promising that he would give this matter his urgent attention, he left the house.

If someone was blackmailing her, it had to be stopped. So far, there had been no demands for money. Could it be kept quiet? Damn, he was sure this incident had passed.

When Betty received the first letter and brought it to him, Jason insisted that it be shown to Max. He had to believe that Max was not involved in this. The man had never lied before, and to Jason's knowledge he felt reasonably sure it was not Max. He prayed it wasn't Max.

Ed Dement was dispatched to assist the President's wife with a personal problem. Since the Director of the Secret Service had personally assigned him, Ed was anxious to find out what the problem was.

When he arrived at the Bethesda residence, where the family was staying through New Years, he was ushered inside. He had seen Betty Stewart's picture in the paper many times, but he was unprepared for the beauty he saw in her face. She had a few lines around the eyes but her smile was radiant. Maturity had been good to Betty, he thought.

Without ceremony, April showed Ed the letters she had received. Clearly she admitted that she was unaware of any secrets that was worth anyone's trouble to expose. She had been faithful to Jason throughout their marriage and there were no problems currently with their relationship.

She related how when she returned to Boulder that she was approached by a man named Sam Carpenter who hinted that they had had some sort of a relationship. April said that to her knowledge, Sam was an old school friend that had taken her to the prom. However, after the introductory meeting, he had not tried to contact her in any way. She would appreciate having the man checked out and if possible, find out if he was the mystery person who had been sending these letters.

Try as she could, April could not come up with any other name that might be suspect. She clearly explained to Ed Dement that she thought this was a ploy to get at Jason. She strongly suspected that the person responsible did not have any information but was trying to get at Jason and the office of the President by using her.

She was unable to give Mr. Dement any names of persons she thought might be suspect. Hundreds, maybe thousands of people had worked to get Jason reelected. No one had sent any hate mail during that time or tried to interfere with his campaign.

Ed Dement listened patiently and then asked to use the telephone. He called his office and asked that a passage be booked on the next available flight to Boulder, Colorado.

When he left the house, he could not help but think that Mrs. Stewart was telling the truth. She and the President had always portrayed a loving couple, even when he was Senator. The whole country rallied to her cause when she was so badly injured. She had obviously tried to return their love by involving herself in every charitable cause possible. Many times people had been helped but were unaware that it was Mrs. Stewart who had been their benefactor.

He sincerely hoped that this assignment would not cause a stink in Washington. Some nut probably thinking he can made a fast buck and scare Mrs. Stewart. After all, didn't everyone have a skeleton in the closet? He prayed he would not find any in hers.

20

SAM CARPENTER

First stop for Ed Dement was the old practice that Betty Stewart's father had shared with a Dr. Sloane. His schedule was tight, but when Ed showed his special agent badge, time was made available.

Ed thanked the kind doctor for seeing him. He asked how well he had known Betty Stewart as a child?

Dr. Sloane stated that he had known Betty since birth. He and her father had gone to medical school together and finally established a practice together here in Boulder.

Ed listened patiently as Dr. Sloane rambled on about Betty's childhood. "George and Mary only had the one child. Their marriage was stormy from the beginning. Betty was placed in private schools at the age of six. When she was home there were fights that no young child should be a party to. Me and my Mildred often took her over the holidays just to keep the peace and assure her a warm loving home atmosphere."

"When she was sixteen she ran away from school and refused to return. That's when she come home to Boulder to live. It was rough, she had no friends in the area. Her mother got drunk and killed herself in a car accident."

"George pampered his little girl from then on. Anything she wanted, she got. What she wanted was love but George didn't know how to show it."

"Because she was the daughter of a prominent surgeon she had some social standing in school. I don't think she ever had a best friend though unless it's that no account trash Sam Carpenter."

Ed Dement's ears perked up when he heard this name. Dr. Sloane continued. "Old Sam was the big man on campus. He played football, track, basketball and was great in all of them. He was a lousy student though. He always seemed to get by by the skin of his teeth."

"Well, he took to dating Betty that very year. Whether she liked him or only liked the attention she got from being seen with him, I don't know. Mildred and I just watched from the sidelines."

"When it came time for Betty to go to college, ole George wrote a recommendation for Sam to attend the Air Force Academy. He had some influential friends in politics, so it was fairly easy to arrange."

"Betty completed her college work and came back home. Sam had failed the academic requirements at the Academy and came back home and ran for local sheriff. I think he thought he would marry Betty and George would support him in whatever useless endeavors he chose."

"George told me that one night Betty came home crying and said it was all over between here and Sam. He was an ungrateful bully and she hated him. She asked her father to help her get a position in Washington, D.C. She wanted to get away from Boulder and especially from Sam."

"Guess you know the rest of the story. She was in Washington only a short time when she writes George that she is marrying the young Senator from Georgia. To say he was surprised would be an understatement. She never dated much when she was here. So, meeting and marrying a man she knew less than six months was quite a shock."

"Course Sam went crazy. He swore she married the other man out of spite. Several of his binges landed him in jail and it's obvious he never forgave her."

"When she came home that last time before the plane crash, she told George that she was having marital problems with her husband. Sam had visited her a while back in Washington. Jason never knew that she met him. George told her to make her choice. It was up to her. She could either put it back together, or get out of it completely."

"That's when she told him she was pregnant, least she thought so. She had had such a loveless childhood, I think she was afraid to have the baby. George said she had come home to ask him to perform an abortion. He refused. You see, Betty though the baby was Sam's."

"Now young fellow, if you let anyone see that in any report, I'll deny saying it."

Ed promised that everything was confidential and would remain that way.

Assured, Dr. Sloane began again. "Well, she cried for a month. She told George he was selfish and cruel. He never wanted her. He and Mary never loved her from the beginning."

"George almost had a breakdown over this. True he had a rough time with his wife, but he truly loved his daughter. Things were very explosive for a while."

"I can honestly say, her last visit here really shook George up considerably. She didn't know he had a weak heart and that she had put a considerable strain on him over this visit."

"After one last big fight over the abortion, Betty called her husband and told him that she loved him and was pregnant and coming home."

"Several times she and Sam went out together. George said he thought this was just her way of getting even with him. He never liked Sam Carpenter."

Shaking hands, Ed Dement thanked Dr. Sloane and left his office. He was confused. The girl he heard described in Dr. Sloane's office did not fit the pattern of the Betty Stewart he had met. She loved the children. She loved her husband. If she didn't, she was the best damned actress ever to hit Washington, D.C. Boy what an assignment!

Ed's next stop was to see Sam Carpenter. This was no problem. He was sitting at his desk in the sheriff's office shooting paper wads into a waste basket. He was a large man that gave the impression he would spit on you if he chose to. There was no gentleness in this man's face whatsoever. Probably as a jock he was a bully, and still is, thought Ed.

Walking over to Sam, Ed shook his hand and said he wanted to speak to him about Betty Stewart.

Sam's eyes widened. "That bitch," he said. "She ain't worth taking time to talk about. Her and me was sweethearts in high school. Then she ups and leaves me and marries some damn big shot in Washington. When things weren't going good, she comes back to Boulder and we start going out again. She tells me her marriage is a mess."

"Well we got pretty intimate, let me tell you. Then she ups and leaves again. She went back to that pretty boy she married from Georgia. Her daddy tells me to stay away from his place while Betty is home. I told him to piss off. If she wants to see me, so be it. There ain't nothing he can do to stop it."

"When I heard about the plane crash, I hoped the bitch would be one of the victims. She deserved to die. Then I hear she's alive."

"When her daddy died and she come back to the funeral, she didn't even say hello to me. I sent a big wreath and was there to help her through this rough time. But, oh no. Last month or so she was here for the big fund raiser, I tried to talk to her. She just put her uppity nose in the air and walked away like I was dirt."

"So, what do you want to know? I'll be glad to tell you that the woman acting like the First Lady ain't nothing but a two timing bitch. I don't need a brick wall dropped on me to know when I ain't wanted. If she don't want to know me, fine. I just washed my hands of her. If she walked in here right now, I'd spit on her."

Ed Dement said very plainly, "Sam have you been in touch by telephone or U.S. Mail with Mrs. Stewart since her last visit here?"

"Didn't I jist tell you Mr. I washed my hands of that bitch. I wouldn't waste the price of a telephone call or stamp on her."

Ed Dement left the Sheriff's office feeling reasonably sure that Sam Carpenter was not the man who had sent those letters to Betty Stewart.

A thought came to him while he was sleeping. Why hadn't he thought of it before? There was some speculation about the plane crash she was in. What if — Oh my God— What if Betty Stewart did die in that crash? What if the woman who came to Boulder for her father's funeral and fund raising really didn't know Sam Carpenter? It was a long shot, but it made more sense than believing the woman he met as Betty Stewart was the same woman the people remembered here in Boulder. Truly, they were worlds apart, or, as speculated before, she was the best damned actress to hit Washington over the last twenty years.

Reaching for the telephone, he called his office in Washington. Talking in great confidence to one of his colleagues, asked him to check on the name and address of the person who sat next to Betty Stewart on the flight that crashed twenty years ago. Yes, it was important. And, it was confidential. Get back to me as soon as you can, he said. Ed was wide awake. He ordered coffee through room service. It seemed a lifetime before his call came through.

Fred Murphy said a girl named April Simmons was in the adjoining seat. She was from a small town in Missouri named Popular Bluff.

Thanking Fred, Ed grabbed his suitcase and checked out of his hotel. He had to get to Missouri. If there wasn't a commercial flight, he would charter a small piper cub. He had to get to Missouri as fast as he could.

There was one flight to St. Louis that had a coach seat vacant. Ed took this seat. He wasn't sure what he would find in Missouri, but he had to unravel the mystery of the behavior displayed by the existing Betty Stewart to the one described by the people in Boulder. He had been an agent for twenty five years and he was a pretty good judge of character. What he had recently learned did not fit the pattern.

Ed managed to cat nap on the plane. He rented a car, got a road map and struck out for Popular Bluff. He prayed that the Simmons family was still in the area.

The first stop was the U.S. Post Office. He asked about a Simmons family who had lost a daughter in a plane crash twenty years ago. The old postmistress said that she knew the family. The father died years ago and the mother was in a local rest home. She fished through some papers and gave Ed the address of the rest home.

It was not difficult to find. The smell of old rotting bodies would lead anyone to the place. God, the law should not allow old people to live so poorly, he thought. Trying not to take deep breaths, he inquired of a Mrs. Simmons.

An unsmiling nurse took Ed back to a shabby room that had very little light. There in a bed that reeked of an unwashed body and urine he saw a frail woman with shocking white hair. Her face was sunken in and the skin seemed to be stretched to its limit just to cover the skull that housed the face.

Walking over to the bed, Ed introduced himself. "Mrs. Simmons," he said. "I would like to talk to you about your daughter April. Do you think you could answer a few questions for me?"

The watery eyes focused on Ed and the old woman replied very quickly. "April is dead. She died in a plane crash a long time ago."

"Mrs. Simmons, I know she was in a plane crash, but could you tell me something about her?"

Mrs. Simmons looked at this man again. "Who did you say you are, and why after all these years do you want to know about my April?"

"Mrs. Simmons, I am a Secret Service Agent from Washington, D.C. and I am trying to find out about every passenger on that airplane. Can you tell me something about your daughter? Tell me why she was on that airplane? Tell me what kind of a girl she was? I want to know anything and everything about her."

"My April was a good girl. But I know she didn't die in that crash." Ed was taken back by this statement.

"Young man, I'll talk to you if you promise you ain't here about the insurance. Me and her dad spent that money years ago on medical expenses. So there ain't no way you can get it back, if that's what this is about."

Ed assured Mrs. Simmons this call had nothing to do with any insurance money.

In a soft almost inaudible voice, Mrs. Simmons said, "I never believed she died. I know they told me she did. My April was too young and too good to die. I jist can't believe she died."

Ed was taken about. Was Mrs. Simmons senile? Was she rambling? He couldn't be sure.

"They brung somebody home here for us to bury. There was a little velvet bag they put some of her things in and give them to me. Them things in the bag weren't April's. I know."

Ed's heart was racing. He didn't want to excite Mrs. Simmons but he was dying to ask more questions. Before he could though, the old woman continued on her own. "My April was a good girl. She loved Max Hartley. They grew up together, you know. She worked day and night to get that son of a bitch elected. She didn't know that I knew she was pregnant. It was Max Hartley's kid. I know it was. Then he dropped her. He met a rich girl in St. Joseph and married her instead. April didn't want to break our hearts and tell us she was pregnant and unwed. So she left us a note, got a bus to St. Louis and took a airplane to Washington, D.C. But in my heart, even though I ain't heard a word in twenty years, I know my little girl ain't dead."

Ed opened his mouth to speak again but realized that Mrs. Simmons had fallen asleep. He walked outside to have a cigarette. He had quit smoking twice before but when he got excited about a case, he started all over again.

He waited patiently for Mrs. Simmons to wake up from her nap. When she did, she looked at him and said. "I'm sorry I fell asleep."

"April was a good girl that loved people. She couldn't stand to see people want for nothin. She worked so hard for Max. She made speeches, just ran his campaign, she did. Her daddy couldn't take her death. He died shortly after we buried her from a broken heart. We had to have a closed casket you know. I been waiting twenty years to hear from her before I die. It ain't like her not to write."

"When I heard old Hartley's wife and kids died, I was glad. I know that's sinful, but I hated what he did to my sweet girl. I wished many times it would have been him."

"If April had married him, he would have been a good person. She wouldn't have let him make promises he couldn't keep. Her influence would have gotten him to the top. I tell you this, cause she was a fighter."

Ed waited for the old woman to rest a minute.

"Mrs. Simmons, do you remember what was in that little velvet bag they brought to you with April's body was returned?"

She rolled her watery eyes towards Ed. "Do you think I am senile? Of course I remember. There was a very expensive gold necklace, a bracelet made of gold, a watch that had diamonds around the face and there was a set of rings. One was an engagement ring and one was a wedding ring. April wasn't married, you see."

"Mrs. Simmons, how do you know these were not April's things?"

Answering with a little more than a little irritation in her voice, she said. 'Why on earth would April have the initial's "B.S." on these items? First, cause my eyes ain't so good, I thought it was "A.S." Then I took it to a jeweler and it clearly said B.S. The wedding ring said B.F. from J.S. 1-17-58. Now ain't that odd? Besides, I just told you April wasn't married."

Ed was so happy he almost blurted out that Mrs. Simmons April was indeed alive. He just thanked her and left the room. Dear God, he had just learned that the President's wife was a imposter. The child that had died recently was probably Vice President Hartley's son. He wasn't sure what he was going to do with this information. One thing for sure, he was telling no one. Not even his boss.

Ed booked a flight back to Washington and would tell his boss he had checked out the leads given him by Mrs. Stewart, but they were dead ends. Then he would take a hot bath and sleep for two whole days. If he got lucky Lucy would be at his apartment and they could make love before he succumbed to sleep.

21

THE TRAIL

Ed Dement was troubled. Those letters were not coming from Denver, and there was never a postmark. He felt reasonable sure that someone here in Washington was the culprit. He had information that he wanted badly to share with Mrs. Stewart, but he could not. It was pathetic though for a woman of such wealth to be giving money away to worthy causes and have her mother live in such deplorable conditions. He had taken a picture of Mrs. Simmons in her filthy room and wanted to have Betty Stewart see it. To do this though would be admitting to her that he knew her identity.

After swearing Lucy to a silence oath, he asked her to have someone from the social services agency contact Mrs. Stewart and show her the picture. Tell her that someone had dropped the picture in the office with the woman's name on it and the name of the rest home she was in.

"Call her on another case, but make sure that Mrs. Stewart sees that picture." Lucy assured Ed that she would do the job herself. She was a social worker and had employed Betty's assistance several times when the wheels of government couldn't provide emergency funds for housing or food for a special client. She currently had a family in desperate need of assistance. Marshals had shown up and moved the family and their possessions out onto the street. While they were trying to contact Lucy, other people had come by and taken whatever possessions they wanted from the litter on the street. Because of the holidays, there were no social agencies open, so they contacted her for emergency assistance. If Betty would assist in the matter, it would be greatly appreciated. If Lucy could come by, Betty would have a check ready for whatever amount she needed to give this family shelter and assure them some food.

Lucy had been to Betty's home several times in the past and was invited into the kitchen where Betty and Daisy were drinking tea. She was invited to join them.

Taking out the folder she had brought along, Lucy showed Betty the history of the family and told her some of the events leading up to their being dispossessed. They were good people, just down on their luck. They were one of the few deserving families, in Lucy's opinion, that needed a helping hand. The father and mother both were willing to work at whatever jobs they could find to keep them going. Recently they had both been laid off and the father had come down with pneumonia. The grandmother had fallen and broken her hip and was unable to watch the children so the mother couldn't work either. Of course they had no savings. They hung on as long as they could before asking for assistance. When they did ask, it wasn't possible to turn the wheels of the government quick enough to keep them from being dispossessed. There were three small children involved, all under six.

April got her checkbook and wrote a generous check for the cause. As they continued to sip their tea and talk about Christmas and New Years, Lucy bumped the folder and sent it sailing onto the floor.

April offered to help her pick it up. Seeing the photo, she looked at it. Lucy was watching her intently. April put the photo back into the other papers and there was absolutely no sign of recognition on her face. She had turned it over thought, but Lucy was sure she paid no special interest to it. Gathering all the papers, Lucy rose to leave. Again she graciously thanked Betty for her generosity. Outside, Lucy said to herself, "Well Ed, you lost that one."

When Lucy told Ed of the event, he said he wouldn't be too sure about Betty's not noticing the name and address on the back of the photo. In a few days, he would simply call the rest home and ask for Mrs. Simmons. If she wasn't there, that would prove a theory he had. Lucy was dying of curiosity, but she knew better than to ask too many questions about Ed's work. If he wanted her to know, she would know. If not, she wouldn't. It was the nature of their relationship. Don't ask too many questions!

Ed had checked into his office, answered a few phone calls and checked his mail. Then he drove over to the archives of George Washington Hospital. When he finally found the records on Betty Stewart, he was amazed at how well the plastic surgery had been performed. Scanning the pictures he saw that the face was a mess. She had no top lip. Her teeth were broken off. Jaw's were broken and her nose was horribly out of place. He appreciated the skill of the man who put it back together where it belonged. Her hair was all matted with blood and there were horrible burns on her hands and neck. He read where her leg and arms were broken, several ribs had been mended. She was indeed a lucky person to have survived the accident. If he thought he would find something here, he was wrong. However, being the methodical person he was about his work, he scanned the medical records and wrote down the names of the nurses and doctors that had access to Betty Stewart at that time. He listed every name. His next task would be to check out every person on that list. He would start with the surgeon and keep going down to even the cleaning people. It would take time and he would leave no stone unturned. The most amazing thing about the letters was, they hadn't made any demands. Usually when a person stoops to this type of extortion, they ask for money. Whoever it was, was either very clever or extremely stupid. Only time would tell. Which secret did they know? Did they know that Betty Stewart was April Simmons or did they know that J.J. Stewart was actually Max Hartley's son? OR, the big question. Did they know the whole secret. And the winner of the blue ribbon would be the person who could answer why they had waited twenty years to come forward? It was a very intriguing case. Usually his cases were boring and he could only recall maybe six in his career that were as interesting as this one. Well, at least he knew why Betty Stewart had acted as she did in the last couple of trips to Boulder. The people who approached her were indeed strangers. She certainly couldn't control what she knew nothing about.

When Lucy left the house that day, it was obvious that April was upset. Where on earth had that girl gotten that picture. There was no doubt that the hardest thing about her whole deception was having to deny that she had a living family. She loved her mother and father dearly, and they her.

Being Jason's wife did not permit April to bring grandparents into their lives. They were supposed to all be dead. This had hurt her over and over not to be able to have them know her children and the children know their loving grandparents.

Max told her at a dinner party that he and Serena had attended April's funeral. Surely her folks had buried her and her memories long ago.

That picture was shocking. Not only that her mother had aged so badly. It seemed to be some place that did not take good care of its senior citizens. Had her mother gone to the home on her own accord? If so, where was her father?

April had seen that the rest home was in Popular Bluff, Missouri. She would simply call Max and ask him to have one of his colleagues check it out for her. She didn't have to say which patient she was interested in. She would tell him about seeing a picture of one of its residents and the conditions were deplorable. It was in his state and he certainly should be interested in these kinds of things. She made a mental note to contact him after he returned from his holiday.

Ed Dement waited patiently for April to tip her hand. He was positive Betty Stewart would not let her mother remain in that horrible place. Time was something he had a lot of. In his job, a man learned patience.

The personnel office of the hospital had given him a list of addresses for the people he had listed in his notebook. His next stop would be to contact someone in the IRS and have them verify the addresses before he went off on a wild goose chase. The one area he always hated to verify was the cleaning people. Many times the employees would work only a short time and quit, get fired, or whatever. Then the company would go out of business. These were the hardest.

Most interesting, was the staff itself. Ed wanted first to approach the nurses who were with Betty around the clock. There were three who had been assigned an eight hour shift while Betty Stewart was in the hospital. Was it possible that she had revealed something while under the influence of medication and now was being blackmailed?

Blackmail kept coming to Ed's mind, but that was the part that didn't complete the puzzle. There had been no demands. When were these people going to make demands? What did they want? Was it, as Betty had said, to get to Jason? Was it to get to Max? The boy was dead. Nothing that surfaced would directly affect him.

Checking into his office, Ed began to make telephone calls to see if he could possibly set up appointments to speak to some of these people. He found six that agreed to meet him in his office. Several were skeptical, but he said he could visit them on their jobs. They could not afford to take time off from work to speak to nobody about nothin. Ed readily agreed. Really, what choice did he have.

He had to give his boss some information about his assignment. He merely said he was following leads that were dead ends. Now he was interviewing people who had been in this hospital when Betty Stewart was a patient. He was given a nod of approval and the Director reemphasized that this was of the utmost secret nature. Anything that could hurt the President, his family or reputation, was to be brought to him first.

Ed nodded that he understood and left to meet with some of the cleaning people.

For the most part, he just got a shake of the head. If they emptied trash or mopped the room where the President's wife was, they were unaware of who she was. Anyway, there was always someone in the room with her when they were there. All they seemed to remember was how awful that poor woman looked with her face all cut, bandaged, and hair shaved where she had something pierce her scalp. Usually, the nurse would just hand them the trash and someone stood by while the bathroom was cleaned or the floor mopped. Since the nurses were bored to death, one would even volunteer to clean the furniture just to have something to do.

Ed talked to five people that day and all said the same thing. He scratched another seven off his list. He sincerely felt he would get nothing more than he already had from them.

Calling it a day, he went home and waited for Lucy to get off work. Ed liked to putter in the kitchen so he made a salad and a casserole and stuck it in the oven. He thought he really should ask Lucy to marry him but he had had one really rotten marriage and didn't want anything to tie him down in his work again. Lucy had been checked out by the Secret Service and found to be a loyal trustworthy citizen. When she suggested they move in together, he had consulted with his boss to assure there would be no repercussions, and then terminated his lease and moved in.

Lucy was wonderful company, a pretty woman to be seen with in public, and great in bed. She made no demands on Ed and that allowed him to move about in his work as freely as he needed to. There was only one problem that complicated this arrangement. Ed had fallen in love with Lucy. He knew it and she knew it. Yet she never pushed or suggested anything other than a continuation of what they already had. What they had was good for both of them.

Max arrived back at the White House rested and felt good for the first time in years. He had spent a glorious week with a woman who was beautiful, attentive, great conversationalist, and ever so wonderful in bed. He sincerely hoped they had been discrete enough so that the press would not blow the whole relationship out of proportion. He hadn't felt that comfortable with a woman since he shunned April Simmons a long, lifetime ago.

It was a surprise when he returned that he found a note on his desk that Betty Stewart had called. She rarely called or consulted with him about anything. Picking up the telephone, he asked her about her holiday. They chit chatted for several minutes, caught up on the latest in each others lives, and then Betty became very serious.

"Max, over the holiday there was a social worker who contacted me about a needy family here in the city. Due to the holidays and shortness of personnel, she asked if I could assist them. Naturally I was more than happy to. However, while she was there, she dropped some papers all over the floor. There was a photograph among them. It showed a picture of an elderly woman in a rest home in your state. It was the Pine Hill Rest Home in Popular Bluff. The conditions shown in this photo were deplorable. Even though the social worker and I did not discuss this person, I have been distraught since seeing it. Couldn't you have one of your trusted employees check this place out and if they are not up to standard, have them shut down, taken to court, or whatever? I would feel so much better if you personally took charge of this for me."

Max assured Betty he would check into the conditions she described and would be in touch with her. Summoning one of aids, he detailed his request and promptly forgot about the situation.

Ed Dement felt as he was standing on top of a beautifully wrapped surprise package and did not know how to get the string off. There was a clue here he had overlooked. He set about diagraming the events. He started with the request from the Director of the Secret Service for him to visit Mrs. Stewart. He added the trip to Boulder. The trip to Missouri. He drew a square showing the chain of people he had interviewed from the hospital. Looking at his diagram, the answer to the puzzle leaped off the page and struck him like a bolt of lightning. Slapping himself on the head, he felt like a fool for letting the most obvious evade him this long. He hadn't included Max's and Serena's families.

Checking out of his office, he got into his car and drove to Haines Point and sat for several hours asking himself if he really wanted to solve this case? Did he want to expose the powerful structure that so peacefully and expertly ran the country. If he could have allowed himself to give in, he would have gone to a bar and gotten falling down drunk. He knew what he had to do and he also knew he would do it. Pushing himself up from the ground where he had been sitting, he got into his car and drove home. He would need a suitcase, some clean underwear and shirts. His burden was still heavy on him.

22

THE FINAL PIECE OF THE PUZZLE

Joan Springer had been on vacation in Europe. Henry had insisted that they return to St. Joseph before the holiday. He hated spending the holidays away from his hometown. True, Serena and the grandbabies wouldn't be there this year, but he didn't want to be in another country during the "season". They had arrived in St. Joseph the second week of December.

Joan was settling in at home and was resting in her bedroom. Her personal maid was unpacking her suitcases and Henry had gone to the office, as usual. That man would never fully retire, she thought. She wasn't sleepy but was tired. She had Patricia bring her some coffee and some assorted pastries. Her downfall was pastry. Because of her consciousness of her weight, she would eat pastry and then diet until she was again size 12. She loved it when people asked her if she and Serena were sisters.

Pat returned with the snacks and an arm load of newspapers and mail. Since Serena and Max had moved to Washington, Joan had taken a subscription to the Washington Post. God forbid that she miss a picture of her beautiful daughter. When Serena and the girls died in the car accident, Joan just didn't cancel the subscription. It was the November/December papers that caught her eye. There was an article about the President's son dying in a car accident on the Rockville Pike and the president being hospitalized.

Several issues later, it showed Max with the Stewart family making arrangements to fly to Georgia and bury the young boy. It was that picture of Jason Stewart Jr. that made Joan let out the gasp. The face on that boy staring back at her was not Jason Jr., but Max Jr.

Joan began to cry. Deep sobs racked her body. Damn that bastard. She hadn't liked the penniless man when Serena became fascinated with him. He didn't have a dime to his name. The college he had attended was far from Ivy League. He knew no one of prominence in the State. He was just a nobody. Many times Joan had tried to persuade Serena not to marry this man. As usual, Serena got her way. Henry pushed the marriage. He went out of his way to introduce Max around. Many meetings were set up by Henry for Max to get to know the old political machine in the state. Joan had given dinner party after dinner party for these occasions.

She had called Serena several times a week while she was in Washington. Even though Serena didn't come right out and say it, there were enough hints to knock the wind out of a sailor that said she was having a difficult time with Max.

Serena's biggest regret was that she had not given Henry the grandson that he wanted so badly. It was true that he had promised to make a grandson wealthy beyond his imagination. Having a granddaughter had been great but Henry still wanted a grandson. He and Serena had many fights over this. She called Henry selfish and asked how he could possibly deny her child because of its sex. In the end, Serena agreed to have another child. Unfortunately, it was also a girl. Henry was livid. He blamed Serena. He blamed Max. He blamed the whole world.

Joan knew that Serena hadn't wanted those pregnancies. She had those children only because Henry insisted. Yet, in her hand, Joan was staring at a clone of Max Hartley. That son of a bitch had been sleeping with the President's wife all along. Serena suspected that Max had been unfaithful, but did not know whom to blame. Certainly she found no fault with herself. She had hired a private detective but they found nothing to report.

"Well, uppity bitch," Joan muttered as she stared at Betty Stewart's picture in the paper. "You'll pay for this, you whoring bitch."

It was with this in mind that Joan told Henry that she needed to make a trip to Washington to do some shopping. She hadn't seen Max for a while and she thought she might drop in on him. Henry could care less. He drove her to the airport and deposited her there. Joan was a good wife, even if she had gotten a little senile, he thought. Her family had been the one with money. Henry had married her for this reason and Joan knew it. Never once in their forty five years of marriage did she ever let him forget it. However, he had prospered though the years and had his business now and didn't need Joan's money. He had worked hard and traveled in the right circles. No one in their right minds bucked Henry Springer unless they wanted a good fight. He was honest, influential, and lived a simple life. Giving in only when Joan became too difficult to live with.

Driving home he wondered if he had been too hard on Serena. He had loved that girl. She was beautiful, intelligent and ambitious like himself. Why had he demanded a heir from his daughter? She was young and healthy. Even after two daughters, she and Max could have tried again. Remorse set it. He felt that he had been badly cheated when fate took his daughter and grandchildren. It was the end of the road for Henry. He'd be damned if he would leave his enterprise to Max. Today, as always when he allowed himself to dwell on this issue, he felt great guilt and remorse. Guilt for pushing Serena too far and remorse for the loss of three beautiful and wonderful people he loved dearly.

Arriving home, Henry was approached by a man who identified himself as a Secret Service Agent. Inviting him inside, Henry poured himself a drink. Ed Dement refused one.

Ed asked his questions concerning Serena and asked Henry just to talk a little about his daughter. Then, Ed asked if Henry knew anyone who would want to expose the President, Vice President or First Lady?

Henry was taken aback. "Certainly not, young man. How dare you ask? Why I am the major reason that Max Hartley got elected in the first place. Without my influence he would still be stuck in some pitiful law firm somewhere defending farmers and handling divorces."

He did mention how disappointed that they were that Serena and Max had not had a son. Henry wanted a grandson badly.

Ed asked to see Mrs. Springer. Henry stated that Joan had just flown to Washington a few hours earlier. She had done this several times this month, he mused. He couldn't understand her fascination with shopping there when St. Louis was right up the road. Her wardrobe was full of beautiful imported clothing she had just purchased overseas. "Guess women never have enough clothes, do they," he commented?

Thanking Henry for his time, Ed drove like a madman to the airport. He felt reasonably sure that when he arrived, Betty would have received another note. Just how Joan had found out, he wasn't sure, but he had to stop her before she did something really stupid and exposed the whole thing to the public.

When Ed got to National Airport he phoned his office and told his secretary to check all the major hotels and find a Mrs. Joan Springer. Maybe she is listed under Mrs. Henry Springer. He was driving over to the White House to see Mrs. Stewart.

Ed fairly took the steps two by two racing up to the First Family's quarters. April welcomed him and asked that he follow her to the study where they could be alone.

While they were settling themselves in, Ed couldn't help but notice that underneath the skilled makeup that April wore, that she was pale. Several times she had apologized when a seizing spell of coughing interrupted their conversation. Her eyes were glazed and she had the look if one who was carrying a high fever. She seemed to have lost considerable weight since he saw her only a few weeks ago.

"Mrs. Stewart," he began. "Have you received any more letters since we last met," he asked?

Reaching into the pocket of her beautiful designer dress, she extracted an envelope. Quietly she said, "This one came today."

As Ed took the envelope and opened it, a piece of paper was unfolded and the words "I know your secret," were clearly typed across it.

With anxious eyes she watched his face. Had he found out anything. What questions could she safely ask this man? Did he have any connection with Lucy's bringing that picture to her house? April's head was splitting and her hands were sweating. Still she sat quietly until her coughing began again.

Ed looked over at her. This woman is seriously ill, he thought. What can I tell her without letting her know that I know?

Quietly he said, "I know the whole story."

April jerked her hand away and tears fairly leaped from her eyes. She began to cry uncontrollably. When she could speak, she said. "I knew it was a mistake to have any part of my life investigated. What are you going to do with this information? Are you going to expose me and my family? Will you allow the knowledge of your investigation to destroy my husband and Max?"

Ed again took her hand. "Mrs. Stewart, I have told no one about my findings, nor do I intend to. However, I think I owe it to you to tell you that somehow Mrs. Springer, Serena's mother sent those notes. She and her husband wanted a grandson so badly. I guess they saw a picture of Jason Jr. in the paper and Mrs. Springer decided you might have been a part of Serena's unhappy marriage. You had to know it was a miserable match.

April dried her eyes, coughed again and looked at Ed Dement. "You have sworn to uphold the law and defend the constitution and to help deter any criminal wrong doing against all persons. How can you withhold this information from your Director? You will lose your position."

"As I have told no one anything about the investigations, I intend, and Mrs. Stewart, I swear to you, I will destroy every note I have by burning them in my own backyard barbecue."

When they both calmed down, Ed agreed to relate all the events to April as he had discovered them. He told her how the people of Boulder had described Betty as a spoiled uncaring bitch. He had talked to Sam and all Betty had done was deflate his ego. She couldn't have known about any past or existing relationship between them. He was wounded, but would survive. Sam was not a factor in the letters.

"It was during the first night at the hotel that I put the switch together. Having met you, I was convinced that you were not acting the part of a loving wife and mother. The obvious answer was, you were not Betty.

"When I visited your mother in that filthy rest home and mam, I want to apologize for using Lucy for that trick. I felt you would want to know. Your mother was given a small velvet bag when April's body was shipped home. Inside was her jewelry and her wedding band was inscribed "To B.F. from J.S. 1-17-58. She also knew that you were pregnant with Max's child when you left Missouri. She said your father died shortly after learning of your death. I asked Lucy to purposely let you see that picture so you could intervene and get your mother out of that filthy place. I didn't know how to come right out and tell you. Rest assured though that Lucy did not and does not know the purpose of that picture. You see we live together and when I get up enough nerve, we are going to be married. I trust her with my life and yours too, but I have told her nothing.

Ed, seeing that April was trying to digest all this information, rose to leave. "Mam, I am going to see Serena's mother from here. The letters will stop, I promise you. Trust me Mrs. Stewart, your secret is safe with me and is still your secret."

Thanking him for all of his assistance, April shook his hand and escorted him to the elevator. She felt relief, but apprehensive. God, she prayed silently, please let him be a man of his word. Before she could walk back into the study, she fainted.

Waking up in George Washington Hospital was a real shock to her. She was hooked up to oxygen and there were tubes in her arms. April was alarmed and seeing a nurse, reached up to remove the mask. "Where am I and why am I here," she asked?

The nurse said she would return shortly with a doctor. She had been waiting for Mrs. Stewart to awaken. April was seized with coughing. It was so hard to breathe. Her chest felt like an old corset pulled too tight.

A face appeared saying he was Dr. Barker and that Mrs. Stewart had pneumonia and bronchitis. Her lungs were so full of fluid that she was extremely fortunate to be alive at this very minute.

Searching the mans young face, April saw the truth. Words could not hide the fact that she was dying. Asking someone to contact her husband and Max Hartley, she fell asleep.

While Max was on the way to the hospital, Jason was paged. He was tied up in a national security meeting and had asked not to be disturbed. His secretary promised that she would inform him of his wife's condition, if it worsened.

Ed went to the Mayflower Hotel and found Joan Springer. He was not surprised to find her in. She had completed her task in Washington by sending the letter to Betty Stewart. Now she was packing to return home.

When Ed introduced himself as a Secret Service Agent, Joan turned white and started to shake. "I didn't mean anything by those letters, honest I didn't. Its just that Henry and I wanted a grandson so badly. When I saw the young boy's picture in the paper, I knew it was Max's son. All I wanted to do was scare her. She had no right to be Max's mistress and have a son. She was the reason Serena was so unhappy. God, what have I done."

Ed felt sorry for the woman sitting on the bed sobbing. "Mrs. Springer, I want you to know that I have to make a report on your sending threatening letters to the wife of the President. Your daughter had an unhappy marriage, that's true, but Mrs. Stewart had nothing to do with that. Jason Jr. was the President's son, not Max Hartley's as you claim. Don't you see, you wanted a grandson so badly, and you are bitter over Serena's death. You are grabbing at straws. Believe me when I tell you again that what you thought it not true. Max was faithful to Serena. We know that she hired a detective to prove him unfaithful. There was no indication of any straying in his report or ours. Now why don't you go home. Henry is waiting for you. Mrs. Stewart does not wish to press charges, so you are free to go. Try to put this all behind you, okay? And I trust that you won't ever speak of this event again. Do I have your word on that?"

All too quickly Joan Springer agreed to never utter one word of her little scheme to anyone. Besides, she would be too embarrassed.

23

THE FINAL CHAPTER

When Max arrived at the hospital, April asked that everyone leave the room. She had to tell Max the truth before it was too late. Her body was failing her fast and she knew that this matter could not be put off any longer.

Signaling for Max to bend down close, April began. "Max I want you to promise me you will take care of Jason. I know I am dying and will never leave this hospital. It's rather funny how I think back about how it all began right here, could even be the same room."

Max was frightened. Why had she so urgently requested him to come here. He leaned close as he saw her lips move again.

"Max forgive me. You were right, I am April Simmons. J.J. was your son. He was so lucky to have two loving fathers. One biological and one who worshiped him and gave him the love he needed to be such a beautiful boy. Now that I am dying, I knew I had to tell you the truth. Please don't hate me. Just remember, it was you who sent me away. I was scared to death, pregnant, and had no one to help me. When Betty switched seats with me on the plane, I had no way of knowing that things would turn out the way they did. I was a young woman protecting her unborn baby the best way she could. Jason was so loving and kind that I decided to begin my deception. Let me tell you, it was the most wonderful decision I ever made in my life. He was a kind and gentle man with so much love to give. I loved that man with a love that could only happen once in a lifetime. I want to thank you Max. Thank you for a wonderful son and for pushing me into Jason's arms. He was my life. I would have done anything to protect them both. He need never know that Betty was carrying another man's child. I don't feel he was cheated though, as he loved J.J. as his own and J.J. loved him as a true father."

Jason had slipped into the room unnoticed and heard his wife's confession. Tears ran down his face. The woman, whoever she was lying there dying would always be the wife he would remember. She was so special. His life had been so empty before she came into it. How he would cope without her would be a real trial. He walked over and kissed her. April opened her eyes and smiled. "Jason Stewart, I love you. Take care of our family and remember me to them often. Thank you darling for such a wonderful life. I can only pray that this conversation will stay inside this room. I never meant to hurt you or have you touched by my scandal." Taking a deep breath, she died in his arms. God knows she would not have wanted it any other way.

April was buried beside her son in the family plot in Georgia as Betty Stewart. Many people mourned her death. Ed Dement burned his report. He merely told his boss that now the President's wife was dead, there should be no more letters. They never posed a threat to the President, only his wife. Immediately he was assigned another case. He would never forget this woman Betty Stewart, or April Simmons. He would always remember her case as the most interesting and challenging he would ever encounter.

For all who knew her, she would be commonly referred to as the Colorado Maiden, loving wife of Jason Stewart and mother of four beautiful children who worked to help all unfortunates who were made known to her. He knew that now she was truly at peace.

ISBN 142514830-1